A Candlelight Ecstasy Romance™

SHE COULD SENSE THE PASSION BUILDING BENEATH THE SURFACE . . .

A passion that would soon break free of its own volition if she did not pull back now. She thought to—meant to—but the intoxicating feel of Cale's mouth on hers made her feel lightheaded, made it impossible for a single coherent thought to form and stay in her mind.

Allison found herself kissing him back without reserve, her mouth moving beneath his, hot and eager for the excitement only he could provide. . . .

O8-BVU-406

AS NIGHT FOLLOWS DAY

Suzanne Simmons

A CANDLELIGHT ECSTASY ROMANCE™

Published by
Dell Publishing Co., Inc.
1 Dag Hammarskjold Plaza
New York, New York 10017

Dell ® TM 681510, Dell Publishing Co., Inc.

Candlelight Ecstasy Romance™ is a trademark of
Dell Publishing Co., Inc., New York, New York.

ISBN: 0-440-10220-0

Printed in the United States of America
First printing—December 1982

To Our Readers:

We have been delighted with your enthusiastic response to Candlelight Ecstasy Romances™, and we thank you for the interest you have shown in this exciting series.

In the upcoming months we will continue to present the distinctive sensuous love stories you have come to expect only from Ecstasy. We look forward to bringing you many more books from your favorite authors and also the very finest work from new authors of contemporary romantic fiction.

As always, we are striving to present the unique, absorbing love stories that you enjoy most—books that are more than ordinary romance.

Your suggestions and comments are always welcome. Please write to us at the address below.

Sincerely,

The Editors
Candlelight Romances
1 Dag Hammarskjold Plaza
New York, New York 10017

AS NIGHT
FOLLOWS DAY

CHAPTER ONE

Closing the door of the dormitory room behind her, the woman gave the knob a good twist to be sure it had locked. Apparently satisfied, she slipped the key into her handbag. She smoothed the skirt of her dress in an unnecessary, nervous gesture and set off down the hall toward the stairway.

Allison Saunders had purposely chosen one of the more understated dresses from her extensive wardrobe for to-night's welcoming banquet. It was a silky creation in burnished gold, which clung to her tall model-thin figure as if it had been made for her, which, in fact, it had. Anyone with a eye for fashion could have quickly discerned the well-known designer's name behind the simple lines of the dress. But Allison reminded herself that New Hampshire in June was hardly New York, thank goodness.

She had deliberately set out to downplay her well-heeled background when packing for the three weeks at Dartmouth College. After all, she was not here as a social-ite or businesswoman, although she had been both in her life. But then Allison had been a lot of things in her thirty-two years. Now she was at Dartmouth as just one more struggling writer attending the summer writers' workshop.

How long had it been since she'd even been on a college campus? The answer came back loud and clear. Ten years. It had been ten years since she had graduated from Sarah Lawrence.

Allison did not need to be told that those ten years had been kind to her, at least in some ways. With hair the shade of gold dust and rather exotic topaz eyes, she scarcely looked her thirty-two years. She had always kept her face and figure in prime condition. No, what troubled Allison went far deeper than mere appearances. She had suddenly realized that she was thirty-two years old and still drifting.

She knew her circle of friends in New York and her family had thought her half crazed the way she had dashed off on practically a moment's notice to attend this workshop. But it had not been nearly as impulsive on her part as it had appeared. The idea had been formulating in the back of her mind for months, and when she finally worked up sufficient courage, she had simply taken off.

She had arrived only the day before in the small New Hampshire town of Hanover, home of one of the oldest institutions of higher learning in the nation. The moment Allison drove onto the campus and parked her Porsche in the student lot, she knew she had made the right decision in coming. That same sense of excitement and wonder that she remembered from so long ago was once more hers. The same feeling of adventure, of going out to conquer the world once again set her heart racing. Admittedly, it was coupled with ten years of maturity, but she would not deny those years even if she could.

She tried to figure out where she had gone astray along the way. She had once been a bright, ambitious twenty-two-year-old who had wanted nothing more than to write, to express her thoughts and feelings and share them with others. Then her life had gotten in the way and she had allowed her dreams to drift away from her. She realized that now. But perhaps it wasn't too late for her, after all. Perhaps there was still time to recapture those dreams.

Allison knew she had no one to blame but herself. While her affluent background may have ruled out the prospect of living the life of the struggling artist, she could still have become a writer if she had dared to try. The fact that her parents had sent her to the best schools, bought her clothes at Lord & Taylor's, and sent her on a European holiday as her college-graduation present was no excuse not to have tried.

Not that she had been idle during the past decade. Far from it. Allison was always involved in one type of venture or another. After her return from Europe, she had taken a position teaching English and creative writing at a private secondary school. In the few hours she could find each week for her own writing, she had worked on a collection of short stories. At the end of the second year, she had discovered that she was no longer interested in teaching and no closer to producing the stories she conceived in her mind and found so difficult to put down on paper.

She drifted back to her parents' home and even became engaged to a boy she had known all of her life. Then one night at a party in New York, Allison had been approached by one of the giants of the advertising industry about a position with his firm. That was the beginning of a new career. And the end of her engagement.

At twenty-four, Allison knew her cultured blond looks were as much an asset to her career in advertising as any skills she possessed. She was at the top of the heap within eighteen months, but her interest soon faded and died. She did what she had always done—she turned her back and walked away with no regrets.

Just as she had managed to turn her back and walk away from two more engagements in as many years, she thought to herself with a wry smile. Allison had never really stuck to anyone or anything for more than a brief time in her entire life.

The next several years had been spent being someone's fiancée or ex-fiancée as she traveled and partied with the New York social set. Her latest venture had been to open an exclusive boutique with a good friend. They had done amazingly well in three years. Then, just a few months ago, Allison had sold out to her partner for a tidy profit. She once again had found herself footloose and fancy-free, with no real direction to her life.

That was when she happened to read in a writers' magazine about the upcoming workshop at Dartmouth College. It had started the germ of an idea in her head. Without a word to anyone, Allison reworked the dusty collection of short stories left over from her days as a young teacher. She recognized the amateurish and sometimes immature quality of many of her stories, but with rare determination she set out to salvage what she considered her best efforts.

It had taken an incredible amount of work just to get her portfolio in order to bring to the writers' workshop.

And there was no small doubt in Allison's mind as to whether she had any talent at all.

Today had been filled with registration and meetings. She had poured over the list of offerings and finally chosen a general-fiction session, one on short-story writing, and one on publishing and editing, skipping over those offered on poetry and nonfiction. She knew there were also manuscript-evaluation sessions, but those came after the first week of classes, which started the next morning. The banquet tonight was the kickoff for the three-week workshop, and Allison was looking forward to hearing the keynote speaker, a renowned woman writer.

For a moment, Allison was afraid. She had taken on this venture with a feeling of life passing her by, and now she wondered what she was doing amidst all of these struggling writers who no doubt had more talent than she could ever hope to possess. She had always approached her life with a rather casual attitude. She was surprised to discover how much this opportunity was coming to mean to her.

Allison reached the staircase and made her way down the two flights to the main lobby of the dormitory. According to the map in the folder presented to her at registration, the dinner was being held in a dining room in the next building. She strolled through the lobby and out into the cool New Hampshire evening.

Allison was gazing about her, appreciating the beautiful campus by the Connecticut River, when a voice nearby interrupted her reverie.

"Hello," said a woman coming up to walk alongside her. "I saw you at registration this morning. You're here for the writers' workshop too, aren't you?"

Allison turned her head and gave the middle-aged woman a smile. "Yes, I am."

"Have you ever been to one of these before?" asked her newly acquired companion.

"No, this is my first," the blonde confessed. "Have you?"

"Yes, I should say so." The woman laughed. "I try to hit a different one every summer. It's like a working vacation for me, but I always come away from these workshops more determined than ever to do something with my writing. By the way, I'm Helen Royce." She extended a friendly hand.

The younger woman returned the firm handshake. "And I'm Allison Saunders."

"It's nice meeting you, Allison," Helen replied, as they resumed their walk in the direction of the dining hall. "Do you mind if I ask what sessions you signed up for this morning?"

"Not at all. I chose three, general fiction, short story, and publishing and editing."

Helen Royce nodded her head as each one was named. "That last session should be particularly useful if you are interested in writing as a career and not just a hobby. I took a similar workshop at Cape Cod last year," she volunteered. "What I learned made the entire week pay for itself."

"This may sound like a naive question, Helen, but are you a professional writer? Have I read anything of yours?" Allison inquired, genuinely interested in the woman's answer.

Helen Royce gave a low chuckle. "I'm afraid not, unless you read *The Toledo Blade.*"

"The Toledo Blade?" Allison had to confess she was not familiar with that particular publication.

"I'm a newspaperwoman," continued Helen. "I have been for more years than I care to admit. *The Blade* is one of our major papers in Toledo. A few years ago, I decided to try my hand at fiction, but it has proven to be a great deal harder to make that switch than I'd anticipated. What about you?"

"I'm strictly an amateur." Allison gave an expressive shrug. "I suppose one of the reasons I'm here is to find out if I even have any talent."

"Aren't we all?" Helen laughed, her dark eyes dancing with amusement. "I have never met a writer yet who didn't ask themselves that question on nearly a daily basis. Even the big names in the field must have their moments and their doubts," she added philosophically.

"Hmm . . . I suppose you're right," Allison murmured. "It must be the artistic temperament."

"That combined with the fact that we seek perfection, and perfection, after all, is only in the mind." The woman paused, realized the dining hall was directly in front of them, and flashed Allison a wry grin. "And that is the end of my lecture, I promise. Are you meeting anyone at the banquet or would you like to join a few of us *seasoned* workshoppers?"

Allison moistened her bottom lip. "I would love to join you, if you're sure your friends won't mind."

"Oh, they won't mind," Helen said briskly with an unshakable confidence that Allison could not help but envy. "None of us had met before this morning, you see."

"You only met this morning?"

At the half-bewildered, half-wounded expression that

flickered across the blonde's finely sculpted features, Helen felt compelled to say more. "Surely you must realize, my dear, that most people will find you rather intimidating at first." She was trying her best to be both kind and honest. "You are a very beautiful woman, Allison. What may actually be a streak of shyness is often interpreted as something entirely different in beautiful people. I am a rather ordinary-looking fifty-year-old. Not much of a threat to anyone—at least on the surface. I think people find us ordinary types more approachable, in the beginning, anyway. Please don't concern yourself. I'm sure the others will quickly discover what I have."

"And what is that?" Allison remarked after due consideration.

The woman gave her hand a maternal pat. "That you are a very nice woman as well as a very beautiful one."

A flush of embarrassed color rose on Allison's cheeks. "I don't think you're the least bit ordinary, Helen Royce."

Helen graciously accepted the compliment as her due. "Thank you." She smiled with a flash of white teeth and a scarcely discernible nod of her salt-and-pepper head. "Are you ready to go in to the banquet now?" she asked in a gentle tone, indicating they had reached the door of the dining room.

"Yes, I'm ready," Allison replied, taking a deep breath.

The two women entered the room side by side, the tall, stunning blonde and the older, graying newspaperwoman. Neither seemed aware of the interest generated by their entrance as they made their way through the crowd to a table at the opposite end of the dining hall.

As they reached their destination, Helen was the first to speak.

"Good evening, everyone," she greeted the half dozen or so people already seated around the table. With a wave of her hand, she indicated that Allison was to take the chair next to the one she intended to occupy herself. "I would like all of you to meet Allison Saunders. Now you'll have to help me with your names," Helen urged in such a way that no one could possibly take offense at her manner. She turned first to the serious young man on her right. "This is Peter Donovan." She went on to introduce the bespectacled woman next in line. "Grace Halsley."

"Hello, Allison," Grace Halsley managed to get in before Helen continued.

"The distinguished gentleman seated next to Grace is Howard Barron, and then there's Michael Polk, Sarah Beall, and to your immediate left is Kate Myers. There! I think that's everyone," Helen concluded, flashing them all a brilliant smile.

An enthusiastic round of applause from the group followed her letter-perfect introductions.

"How ever did you do that?" murmured Allison as they took their places.

Helen waved as if it were of little consequence. "I suppose it comes from being in the newspaper business all these years. You develop a certain knack for remembering people's names."

"I guess so!" exclaimed the younger woman, suitably impressed.

"Where are you from, Allison?" It was Kate Myers who addressed her first.

"I'm originally from Scarsdale, New York, but I've been living in Manhattan for a number of years now," she replied. "What about you?"

The befreckled redhead gave her a big grin and responded. "Nowhere as exciting as New York, I can tell you that. I come from a small town in Illinois. In the summer I try to convince myself I'm a writer. The rest of the year I'm a high-school teacher."

Allison's face lit up with a sense of camaraderie. "I was a high-school teacher for a couple of years. It's been quite a while now. I taught English and creative writing."

"Gosh, I would never have taken you for a teacher," Kate blurted out, her gaze taking in Allison's chic appearance.

The blonde permitted a small sigh to escape her perfectly made-up mouth. "I'm afraid that was always one of my problems. I didn't look like people's idea of a teacher. I suppose I don't look like most people's idea of a writer either. It makes it a little difficult to be taken seriously sometimes."

"I hadn't thought of it that way," Kate Myers confessed, taken aback for a moment.

"I like that about writing, actually," Allison continued. "It is a profession where what we are, or who we are, really doesn't matter. We are judged solely on the quality of the writing we produce."

"You aren't naive enough to believe that, are you?" interjected the scowling young man beside Helen.

Allison recalled that he had been introduced as Peter Donovan. She wasn't sure she cared for the tone of his voice.

"Now, Peter, don't get all over Allison. There must be dedicated young writers in our field, but they really shouldn't jump all over the rest of us." Helen quickly stepped in to act as referee. "Peter is a serious poet, Allison. He thrives in an atmosphere of squalor and deprivation for his art. Isn't that what you told me this morning, my dear man?" Helen turned her clear, dark-brown eyes on him. "Just because some of us support ourselves by working in other fields while we write in our spare time doesn't mean we are any less serious about our *art.*"

"Oh, boy, it looks like a real knock down drag out fight this time," Kate speculated under her breath. "People tend to underestimate a woman like Helen just because she looks like someone's mother. I believe Peter may find he has bitten off more than he can chew in this case." She seemed to relish the possibility.

"But Helen told me that you all scarcely know each other," Allison felt compelled to point out.

"That's true, but most of us have been to these summer workshops before. You soon learn to spot the different types who attend them. Now, Peter is the type who takes himself very seriously. The man has absolutely no sense of humor. That's like waving a red flag in front of someone like Helen who has been around for a long time and has pretty well seen it all."

"Are they actually angry with each other?" Allison inquired as the intense young poet and the feisty newspaperwoman went after each other, seemingly without mercy.

"Good heavens, no." The redhead laughed. "That's half the fun of these college workshops. It gives us the chance to argue back and forth with people who understand what drives us to write, sometimes for years without any tangible results to show for it. Helen is loving every minute of this, and Peter will only come out of it more dedicated and more deadly serious than ever."

19

"I'm certainly glad you're here to explain the rules of the game to me," Allison said, a slow smile transforming her face into a poet's dream. "We really should have a program of the players as well."

Kate responded with a delighted chuckle, her eyes dancing merrily with amusement. "You have a good point there. Be sure to suggest it at the end of the workshop when they ask for ways to improve the sessions."

Their attention was diverted by the arrival of student waiters serving dinner. It appeared to be some kind of steak and a baked potato, preceded by an unappetizing salad of mixed greens.

The group focused on their meal, the conversation becoming more congenial. Allison picked at her steak, too excited to do her food justice and disciplined by years of watching every bite that went into her mouth.

She turned to Kate as they lingered over coffee and cherry torte. "I'm really looking forward to hearing our speaker tonight, aren't you?"

"Who wouldn't be?" exclaimed the man across from them. Allison was finally able to place him as Michael Polk. "Having Christian Trent as a speaker is a real coup for this workshop."

Allison looked at him for a moment, genuinely puzzled. "Christian Trent? But I thought the keynote speaker was . . ." She named the well-known woman novelist scheduled for the evening's program.

"She *was* the original speaker, but I heard her connections got fouled up somehow and she couldn't make it," volunteered Kate. "It seems Christian Trent is here on campus doing research for his next book and agreed to fill in."

"Then this is a coup," Helen interjected. "It's a well-known fact that Christian Trent doesn't usually do this kind of thing. He has always been publicity shy, right from the beginning of his career."

"Christian Trent." Allison repeated the renowned novelist's name, conjuring up the titles of three blockbusters that had taken the literary world by storm in the past five years. Little was actually known about the man, but it was rumored that at his current pace Christian Trent would be a candidate for a Pulitzer prize before he was thirty.

There were never any carefully posed photographs of the author on his book jackets and no biography beyond a few vague statements. It was obvious that the man intended to keep his personal and professional lives separate. Christian Trent had been one of the great mysteries of the publishing world for several years. No one seemed to know much about him and those who did weren't talking. It was indeed a coup to have him speaking at the workshop.

"The man writes strictly for the commercial market," scoffed Peter.

"Surely being a commercial success is no sin," Helen responded. "You must admit his novels are far and above the usual sort of tripe that makes the best-seller list."

"I don't read best sellers." Peter sniffed with some sort of misplaced pride.

"You can't judge a man's work if you haven't even read it," Allison finally spoke up. "Christian Trent is a fine writer. He shows a genuine sensitivity for people in his novels. The way he writes is almost a form of poetry in itself."

"Bravo, Allison," Helen murmured under her breath.

Allison was warming to her subject now. "I believe Mr. Trent writes about real people and real feelings without resorting to the kind of sensationalism that so many popular novelists seem to employ. I would give anything to be able to write the way he does." Her cheeks were slightly flushed when she finished.

"I know I would," piped up Michael Polk from his side of the table.

"Well, it should be interesting to hear what the much-debated Mr. Trent has to say to us tonight. Since none of us apparently knows what he looks like, it is entirely conceivable that he is in this room now." With that comment from the normally reticent Howard Barron everyone at the table began to surreptitiously glance over his companion's shoulder to see if any one could spot what appeared to be a young and successful writer. They all came up empty-handed.

"It would seem that Mr. Trent has not joined us for dinner," Helen suggested, tongue in cheek. "We will all simply have to wait to catch a glimpse of the celebrated Christian Trent."

The remainder of the dinner was spent discussing Trent's three best-selling novels. Each of them seemed to have their personal favorite, and everyone but Peter was of the opinion that the evening's speaker was going to be quite extraordinary. Kate even suggested, half in jest, that the elusive Christian Trent deliberately sought to keep his identity secret because he did not measure up to the image the public had formed of a man who wrote such strong, sweeping novels.

But Allison was quite sure that his strong, powerful stories and characters came from an equally strong, pow-

22

erful man. If such a man existed today, that is. She had always imagined him to be one of the rugged individualists that Ayn Rand had immortalized in her novels.

When the dinner was concluded and the dishes cleared away, Dr. Edmund St. John, the head of the Dartmouth summer workshop, came to the podium at the front of the room. He made a few welcoming remarks and then introduced the staff that would be teaching and evaluating the work during the next three weeks. Then the moment came everyone had been waiting for. Dr. St. John explained the great honor that had been bestowed upon them and without further ado yielded his position to Christian Trent.

There was just the briefest moment of suspenseful silence. Then out of the shadows to one side of the dining room a great bear of a man rose to his feet. He reached the podium in one long, lithe movement and stood there for a moment or two looking out over the assembled group. Then with a wry smile directed at himself as much as at his audience, he began to speak.

Allison found herself enthralled with the voice and the man. Christian Trent was just as she had imagined he would be, a larger-than-life character. If she was any judge, he stood no less than six feet four inches tall and tipped the scales at two hundred twenty pounds. His hair seemed to have a life of its own. Worn on the longish side, it was the color of roasted chestnuts by firelight. Allison couldn't be certain of the eyes at this distance, but they appeared to be golden brown and long-lashed.

This was a man obviously in his prime. His John Wayne shoulders, lean hips, and narrow waist were all shown to their best advantage in a dark suit, which somehow seemed not to be his usual attire. Allison suspected he was more at home in a pair of jeans and a sweater.

There was not the slightest hint of softness about Christian Trent. He looked more like a lumberjack than a writer, an outdoorsman through and through. His rugged features showed that he might well have lived the life of hard work and adventure so richly described in his novels.

Allison was spellbound not only by his looks and his deep, resonant voice, but by what she thought she knew of Christian Trent from his books. As any reader would, Allison wondered how much of the writer went into his work.

Then a strange feeling crept over her, a sense of déjà vu. Something in Christian Trent's manner, something about his looks, made her feel as if she had known him before. Allison stared at him intently, secure in the knowledge that the entire audience was doing the same thing. She finally marked it down to her familiarity with his writing, but as he spoke a nagging doubt still persisted in the back of her mind.

She couldn't help but wonder, too, why he chose to remain a recluse. He was a wonderful speaker, unlike so many she had heard. He spoke with conviction that was beyond doubt, stirring the imagination, yet with a sardonic wit that left them all laughing.

Allison kept pushing the thought that she knew this man out of her mind, but it returned again and again to haunt her. The name Christian Trent meant nothing to her, and yet there was something in his tall, broad frame, his eyes, his manner of speaking that seemed vaguely familiar.

She tried to sort through her memories of names and

faces, determined to find the key, but it was to no avail. She had met so many people over the past few years. She was quite sure if she had met this man she would remember the occasion.

Trent kept his speech short, but packed it with information and insight. A burst of enthusiastic applause followed when he finished. He gave a slight nod of his head and a deep, rumbling grunt and went back to his seat.

Dr. St. John once more approached the podium. He extended his thanks to the speaker and then invited the entire group to meet the members of the staff and Mr. Trent at the conclusion of the evening.

"Well, now, that is unusual," Helen commented to Allison after a general buzz started up around the room. "I wonder if Edmund St. John is a personal friend of Christian Trent's. I never thought I would have the opportunity to meet a writer of his stature when I signed up for this workshop, I'll tell you that." She was obviously pleased at the prospect. "Would you like to join the line once the initial fervor dies down a little?"

The younger woman paused for a moment. "I don't know," she finally admitted. While meeting Christian Trent was a once-in-a-lifetime opportunity, she still hesitated. Allison knew it had something to do with her strange feeling.

"Don't tell me after the way you flew to his defense you aren't interested in meeting him?" Helen regarded her with an expression of disbelief.

"Oh, no, I would love to meet Mr. Trent," Allison quickly reassured her companion.

"And so would I," interjected Kate with a faraway look

in her eyes. "As my students back home would say, the man is a real hunk."

"Yes, he certainly is large," Allison murmured thoughtfully. "Do you happen to know by any chance if Christian Trent is his real name?" An idea began to form in her mind. Perhaps that would explain why she felt she knew him and yet could not place his name in her past.

Helen deliberated for a minute and then shook her head. "I honestly don't know. I always assumed that was his real name, but you know as well as I do that many writers do use pseudonyms."

"Considering his well-known aversion to publicity, it is entirely possible he uses a pen name," offered Kate, staring across the room. "Whatever his name, I intend to shake his hand and give him my best smile."

"You and every other female in the room." Helen laughed. "I'm not so old that I can't appreciate Mr. Trent's obvious attractions, you know."

"Well, then, what are we waiting for?" sighed the redhead, unconsciously straightening her shoulders.

"Are you coming with us, Allison?" Helen inquired in a brisk tone as she and Kate got to their feet.

"Yes . . . of course," she replied with a strange air of distraction. Allison eased her chair back from the table and gracefully rose to follow their lead.

Her attention was not required again until she found herself shaking hands and exchanging greetings with the first staff member in the informal receiving line. Allison smiled absently and moved on to the next person, all the while conscious only of the man standing at the end of the line.

Allison had always prided herself on knowing how to

meet people in any situation. She had done a great deal of it since she was a girl. At thirty-two, she was the end product of a gracious upbringing that stressed good manners. But tonight was an exception to that rule. All she could think of as she met the staff members was the moment she would come face to face with Christian Trent.

She could feel the tension and suspense build within her as she looked out of the corner of her eye and realized she was only several people away from him. She was fully conscious of the moment Kate shook his hand and flashed him the promised smile. She was even more aware of Helen and Christian Trent exchanging pleasantries. He seemed to spend more time talking with Helen than anyone else who had passed through the receiving line.

And then the moment came when Allison stepped up to shake hands with Edmund St. John, who was introducing each person to the big man at his side. She smiled at Dr. St. John and opened her mouth to give him her name when an even bigger hand reached out to take hers.

"Miss Saunders and I are old friends," declared the deep male voice as she gazed up at the man who towered over her.

Allison stared into the golden-brown depths of his eyes for what seemed like minutes. Then her own eyes went wide with surprise and recognition as the mystery at last unraveled itself. Her face changed with startling suddenness. "Cale? Cale Harding? You're Christian Trent?"

"Yes, Allison, I am Christian Trent," the man said with a faint cynical smile.

CHAPTER TWO

For a moment, Allison found she could not speak. She was stunned to discover that Cale Harding was the renowned author Christian Trent. Her eyes studied the angular planes of his face, now seeing the familiar lines that told her it must indeed be true.

"I can't believe it," she finally murmured in a hoarse voice. "I mean, I *do* believe you're Christian Trent, of course. It's just that it is somewhat of a shock." She felt she was expressing herself poorly and was irritated by her lack of composure.

"I assure you, it is true." The man grinned, his straight white teeth in sharp contrast to the deeply tanned skin of his face. "You didn't recognize me right away, did you?" he added with an inclination of his head.

"No, I didn't. But I did have a strange feeling that I should know you." She hurriedly went on. "You must admit you've changed a great deal since the last time I saw you."

"Yes, I suppose I have at that." Cale laughed. "Ten years is a long time. You don't seem to have changed that much—except that you're more beautiful than ever." Allison flushed like a girl under the scrutiny of his intense gaze. It was an odd sensation to have him speak to her as one adult to another. "I assume you are here at Dartmouth for the writers' workshop," Cale continued as he finally released her hand.

"Yes, I am," she replied. Allison glanced behind her at the people still impatient to meet Christian Trent. "I think I'm holding up the entire line. Perhaps I should be moving on."

"Why don't you wait for me? I'll be finished here in a few minutes and then we can talk. We have a great deal of catching up to do, Miss Saunders," he said in a quiet and determined voice.

"All right," she agreed after the briefest of pauses. She was a little intimidated now that she had discovered just who Cale had become.

"Good. I'll be with you as soon as I can," Cale stated categorically. Then he turned his attention to the man behind her.

Allison moved away from the receiving line and wandered back to her table. Kate and Helen stood waiting for her. They were both openly curious about her rather lengthy conversation with Christian Trent.

"Whew, what was that all about?" Kate burst out laughing, but broke off at the sight of Allison's thoughtful face.

"It seems Mr. Trent had a great deal to say to you, my dear," prodded Helen, gathering up her evening bag. At the blonde's apparent reluctance to answer, she went blithely on. "I believe the dinner and festivities are fairly well concluded. Kate and I were thinking of taking a stroll around the campus before we return to our rooms. Would you like to join us?"

Allison hesitated for a minute, then realizing that her behavior was silly, she put her chin up and looked at her two companions. "I'm afraid I can't join you. I'm meeting someone in a few minutes."

"Oh . . ." Helen regarded her with an odd expression on her normally composed features.

"You're meeting Christian Trent," Kate ventured with surprising accuracy.

"Yes, I am, but how did you know?" Allison's forehead creased a moment.

"It just made sense somehow," the other woman replied enviously but without malice.

"It's not quite what you are thinking." Allison sought to correct the impression they both seemed to be harboring. "Cale—Mr. Trent and I knew each other some years ago. I thought there was something vaguely familiar about him, but with a different name and having changed so much, it took me awhile to place him."

"You knew Christian Trent?" Helen repeated. "I can't imagine forgetting a man like that."

"He was much younger when I met him. Believe me, he has changed drastically," Allison explained.

Kate drew her thickly marked brows together in a suggestive manner. "So . . . you and Christian Trent are old friends. . . ."

"It's not what you're thinking," Allison repeated herself with weary emphasis. She realized full well the woman meant no harm or offense. Knowing the truth, she began to bite the corners of her mouth against a smile. "You know, Kate, you have a suspicious mind for a high-school teacher from a small town in Illinois."

Kate blushed a shade of red to match the color of her

hair and grinned sheepishly. "It comes from spending most of my time with teen-agers. But how *do* you know the man?" she persisted, apparently determined to get to the bottom of it one way or another.

Allison seemed uneasy for a moment, then cleared her throat and replied, "Well, if you remember, I told you I had been a high-school English teacher for a couple of years some time ago. The first year I taught I had Christian Trent in one of my classes."

"You mean to tell me that you were Christian Trent's high-school English teacher!" Kate reiterated, her eyes wide with astonishment. She burst into a rollicking round of hysterical laughter. "I don't believe it! You scarcely look old enough to have been anyone's teacher and you're telling us that you taught that huge hunk of a man over there?"

"It's not that funny, Kate," Helen interceded. "Please go on, Allison. I'm dying to hear the rest of your story." She bestowed a withering glance upon their companion.

"It really isn't much of a story. Christian Trent"— Allison still found it difficult to reconcile the two names in her mind—"was a senior in one of my creative-writing classes. I was just out of college and awfully green, I'm afraid. I don't suppose I could be more than four or five years older than him." That last comment was directed at Kate. While Allison realized that the idea of her being Trent's teacher might seem incredible now, they had not known Cale Harding as she had. He had been quite different as a high-school student. A tall, skinny eighteen-year-old with a mop of unkempt hair and hungry, defiant eyes. That was the way she remembered him. Yes, he had been very different then.

31

"I think it's fantastic!" Helen responded enthusiastically. "Imagine one of your former students going on to become a world-famous author. Did he have talent even back then?" she asked curiously.

"Yes, he honestly did," Allison said, revealing that much to them. "Of course, I wouldn't say he had the skill or technique he does today, but the signs were all there even at eighteen."

"That has to be one of the most amazing tales I have ever heard," quipped Kate. "Just think, Christian Trent's teacher. I wouldn't mind volunteering for the job now." She grinned broadly.

"I'm sure the man has had more volunteers than he can count," the older woman returned in the dry, brusque voice of experience. "And I'll warrant if there is any teaching to be done these days, it's Christian Trent that does it." That seemed to be the final word on the subject as far as Helen was concerned. "I can certainly understand now why you aren't going for that stroll around campus with us," she bantered. "We'll no doubt see you in the morning for breakfast."

"No doubt," echoed Allison, feeling there was no need to tell the woman she didn't eat breakfast. "Thank you for including me in your group tonight," she added with sincerity as the two women took their leave of her.

Once Kate and Helen had gone, Allison helped herself to the lukewarm remains of her coffee, settling at the empty table to await Cale Harding. She occasionally glanced up at the thinning line and attempted to calm her own rather jittery nerves. It was quite ridiculous to be nervous, she told herself. The man was a former student she had not seen in nearly ten years, or was it nine? Anyway, she was being downright silly and that was more than a little ridiculous at her age.

Yes, but this was not the Cale Harding she recalled from Park Academy, a small inner voice reminded Allison. He had been just a talented kid in those days. Now he was a world-class writer and very much a man.

Under the guise of staring into her coffee cup, Allison studied the man standing halfway across the dining room from her. Sometime over the intervening years, Cale had added the necessary weight to transform him from a bean-pole into one of the biggest men she had ever known. His broad shoulders made anything or anyone behind him impossible to see. And she had the feeling that his growth had not all been physical.

Cale was a man now, not a boy, and he was famous. Suddenly, it all seemed hopelessly embarrassing to Allison. She wasn't even sure what they would have to talk about. There was little doubt in her mind, though, that Cale Harding as Christian Trent could intimidate the devil himself.

She watched with interest as a pretty young woman spoke to him, her body leaning toward him in an unconscious gesture. Or was it really so unconscious at that? There was no mistaking the fact that Cale possessed the kind of latent sensuality that attracted women of nearly any age. No doubt they all hoped to soften the rather hard and sometimes cynical expression that seemed habitually to occupy his features.

Allison thought back to what she knew of Cale as a student. He had been at the exclusive Park Academy on an academic scholarship, that much she recalled. His clothes had been those of a boy who could ill afford the

33

tuition on his own. She had the vague notion that his family, if there had been one, had pretty much left the boy on his own as well.

That brought back the memory of a conversation she had had with him about attending college. If he didn't get a scholarship and a guarantee of a part-time job, it would be impossible for him to even consider college. Cale had informed her of that fact in no uncertain terms. When she had inquired if his parents wouldn't be able to help him with the expenses, the boy had clammed up and had never spoken of it again. Allison wondered if Cale had ever managed to acquire the education he had so desperately desired.

That seemed to open up the floodgates of her mind and the memories came rushing in, memories she had not thought about in years. Somehow the youthful Cale Harding and her own dreams and ambitions as a young woman were stored in the same memory bank. She had been so full of plans in those days. To have allowed them to slip through her fingers without a fight was a sobering thought. It was not easy to admit that she had wasted years pursuing pastimes instead of going after the real thing.

There had been a time in her mid-twenties when Allison had assumed she would find that one man and build her life around his. That had not turned out to be the case. She supposed her three engagements were more than ample proof of that. At least she had learned to quit making formal announcements concerning the men who came and went with some regularity. She had not found that one man, but she had come to realize the only life she could build was her own.

The fact most people failed to understand was that Allison Saunders was basically a shy woman. It was assumed that because she was beautiful, she must be an extrovert. Actually, nothing could have been further from the truth. Beneath the layers of carefully acquired sophistication, Allison was something of an introvert. Being pretty had been a hindrance as well as a blessing. She had been sincere when she confessed to Kate that her looks made it difficult for her to be taken seriously. It was the one thing she wished she could change about her life, and it was the one thing she was incapable of changing.

Allison sat for some time deep in thought. It was odd how her own past and Cale Harding's seemed to be woven together like two strands of the same thread. And it was odder still that they should meet again after all these years under the present circumstances.

Lost in her daydreams, Allison was visibly startled when a deep masculine voice, a voice that had changed over the years and yet in some ways was the same, sounded her name.

"Allison, are you ready to go?" Cale looked down at her with a curious expression on his rugged features.

"Yes," she murmured, forcing herself out of her reverie, "I'm ready to go." Allison rose to her feet. Cale's hand on her elbow expertly steered her from the dining room.

"I thought we might go for a walk." Cale stated his intentions with an easy smile.

"That's fine with me," she replied, permitting him to determine the direction in which they headed. "You certainly have come a long way since the days when we were both at Park Academy," she ventured, unsure of just where to begin a conversation with a stranger who was not quite a stranger.

"Yes, I have come a long way," he replied, making no attempt at false modesty.

"Did you ever get to college?" Allison inquired, eager to satisfy her curiosity. "I seem to recall we talked about it once. I've always wondered what happened to you, Cale." She felt some inexplicable need to expound on her own question, although it was a perfectly natural one for a teacher to ask a former student.

"I'm surprised you remembered." Cale frowned, apparently absorbed in his own thoughts for a moment. "As a matter of fact, I did attend college."

"I should have known you would manage. You always did know how to go after what you wanted," she said, a small smile playing at the corners of her mouth as she glanced up at him.

The hardest thing for Allison to reconcile in her mind was the boy she had known with the man now walking beside her. The fact that she was aware of him as a handsome and obviously virile male did not help matters. It only complicated them. The subject of Cale Harding was a paradox that left her feeling strangely at odds.

"I got the scholarship I needed," he continued, "and even managed to graduate with some kind of distinction. To my knowledge, I offended only those professors whom I least liked in the process." He chuckled from deep within his throat. It was a dark sound that hovered on the night air and echoed off the nearest building, coming back to Allison's ears a second time rather eerily.

"You always were something of a rebel, Cale Harding," she pronounced with a touch of reproach.

Cale threw his head back and let out an unrestrained, giant-size roar of laughter. "Once a teacher, always a teacher, eh, Miss Saunders? I had forgotten how you could put us in our place with that subtle suggestion of disapproval in your voice." Then he laughed again. A long, rich, deep laugh.

"I'm glad you find it so amusing now, Mr. Harding," she said, a shade haughtily. "If I remember correctly, you would not have dared to laugh in the old days." Suddenly, Allison wasn't sure she liked being reminded of their former relationship. It made her feel old somehow, and that was a new experience she found she didn't care for one bit.

"Then, thank God, the old days are long gone and we're just a man and a woman who once knew each other for a few months. I must admit that while I admired you as a teacher, I much prefer you as a woman," Cale stated, looking down at her with a curious expression on his face. "But what about you, Allison? What have you been doing all this time? I seem to recall you were doing some writing yourself when you were teaching at Park Academy."

"I never did do much with my creative writing after I left teaching," she confessed reluctantly. "I got involved in other things, and it has been just recently that I have had the opportunity to try my hand at it again."

"You were in advertising for a while, weren't you?" he commented, looking out across the stretches of green lawn that glistened with the evening dew. "I saw your name in a magazine a few years back."

"I was in advertising for a couple of years. It was fun for a while, although it was incredibly hard work, too. It was never something I really wanted to do and so eventually I quit."

37

"What have you been doing since then?" he pressed, steering her down a sidewalk to their left.

"I started a business in New York with a friend of mine. I've been involved in that until recently. I sold out my half of the partnership and here I am." Allison's poor attempt at flippancy fooled neither of them.

"I see . . ." Cale muttered as if he were trying not to pass judgment on what she had told him.

"What about you, Cale?" Allison felt it was his turn to talk and hers to listen.

"I worked for a year after I graduated from Park Academy. There were circumstances at home that made it impossible for me to go to college right then. Fortunately, I did receive a scholarship and the following fall I was able to take advantage of it. I went to Yale, you know."

"No, I didn't know," she admitted. "I left Park the following year myself. I had no idea what had become of you until I saw you tonight," she conceded.

"That must have seemed doubly odd then," Cale said in a low voice. "At least, I knew something about what had happened to you. Quite honestly, you have changed far less than I have since those days at the Academy."

Allison heard herself chuckle at that. "You can say that again!" she exclaimed, glancing up at the man's tall, powerful form. "You are definitely very different from the boy who was in my creative-writing class."

Cale studied her for a moment with something akin to humor flickering in his golden-brown eyes. "Now that I've seen you again, Miss Saunders, I can only say 'thank God!'"

Allison felt a strange shiver course down the arm still entwined with his. She had never thought of Cale Harding in a sexual way when he had been a student of hers, but there was no denying the signals she was receiving now. And why not? They were both adults, and he was a very attractive man, both physically and intellectually. She felt as if she almost knew how his mind worked from reading his books. It was suddenly as if the tall, thin boy she had once known no longer existed.

She would be the first to admit that part of the attraction was due to the fact that she had always been enthralled with Christian Trent's writing. His books were about strong, intelligent, yet sensitive people. And his love scenes were surprisingly sensuous for a male writer, all too many of whom wrote rather mechanical sex scenes.

Allison half feared that her attraction to Cale would be blown out of proportion if she confused his characters with the man himself. It did not necessarily follow that the men he wrote about represented Cale Harding. But deep inside, Allison knew somehow that they were the same and would always be so for her.

It was only because he was a writer that she could feel she understood his attitudes about life and love and death without ever having actually discussed those things with him. If Cale Harding were half the man she imagined him to be, then he was indeed someone very special.

Allison glanced at him out of the corner of her eye and discovered that he, too, was watching her with interest.

"Tell me, Allison, have you ever married?" he finally asked in that resonant voice of his that she was quite sure would be imprinted on her memory for the rest of her life.

"No . . . I never married." She gave a funny little grimace. "I . . . ah, I considered it several times, but it never seemed to work out. Have you?" She turned the question back to him.

"Hell, no. I suppose I haven't had the time or inclination," he explained. "At the beginning of my career I was too caught up with my writing to consider a permanent relationship with a woman, and I was dead broke to boot. With success came a different set of problems that I'm sure you must have encountered as a beautiful, successful woman in a high-powered field like advertising."

"Yes, I did," she murmured thoughtfully. "Sometimes a name or face can be a hindrance rather than a blessing. There are always those people who collect other people like they were ornaments of some kind. Do you know I finally had to get an unlisted telephone number when I was at the height of my career just to avoid the weird calls I was getting? There were even times when I wondered if a man was asking me out because of the person I was or because of my looks. I think that was what drove me to quit the business. That and the fact that I felt like I was shriveling up inside. It's not an easy profession in which to keep some kind of perspective about yourself." Allison found herself confiding in Cale as she had never done with anyone before. She sensed somehow that he would understand what she was trying to say.

"Damn, don't I know it!" he muttered, half angry and half amused. "For me it got so bad for a while that I even began to suspect that a woman was willing to go to bed with me just to see if I lived up to the image of prowess I wrote about in my books. Either that or it gave her something to brag about to her friends or the gossip columnists. It pretty well turned me into a hermit the past couple of years. When I'm working on a book I tend to be something of a hermit, anyway."

"I understand you're researching a new book now." Allison broached the subject with care.

"Yes, I am, but how in the hell did you know that?" Cale regarded her with a slight suggestion of suspicion.

"I . . . I didn't mean to pry," she stammered, wishing she had never brought it up. "Someone mentioned it at the dinner tonight, that's all. They said you were here at Dartmouth doing research and that was no doubt why you agreed to speak at the banquet."

"Well, at least that is one story that hasn't been exaggerated beyond any semblance to the truth," Cale hissed through his teeth. "I am here using the library facilities, and I did agree to speak when Edmund St. John approached me and explained his problem." Cale paused and then added censoriously, "I don't usually give speeches. They're a damn waste of time. There's nothing I can say in twenty minutes that is going to help someone else become a writer. The only way to do that is by hard work and by writing and more writing." His opinion of such activities was made all too apparent to Allison.

"Perhaps not," she conceded, "but you do inspire other people whether you know it or not. You inspire them by your success and by your very presence. Even if it motivated just one good writer not to give up in frustration, wouldn't it be worth it? I thought your speech was wonderful and so did everyone there tonight." Her face lit up as she spoke. Cale stopped and looked down at her from his towering height.

"Well, I must say that is high praise coming from you," he said with unusual warmth.

41

But Allison had the distinct impression that he could not care less whether he inspired anyone or not. Cale Harding was an even more complicated character than the ones he drew so vividly with his pen. She was beginning to see that quite clearly.

"You deliberately use a pseudonym, don't you?" she ventured, thinking she understood his reluctance to use his real name.

"Sure I do. I would never get any peace if everyone knew who I was," Cale replied as if he thought her a little naive about the whole thing. "I sell what I write, Allison. I don't sell myself. I don't mind in the least if Christian Trent is a household word, but I wouldn't want Cale Harding to suffer that same fate. What most people fail to recognize is that the two are not the same man. I suppose in a sense I'm a split personality."

"I think I understand," she murmured empathetically.

"Then you do understand the need for privacy. It is unique to some professions that people tend to confuse the public person with the private person. I believe that is true in any business that is essentially entertainment or in the business of selling—whether it's a face or a book."

Cale slipped a sympathetic arm around Allison's shoulders as he spoke, somehow sensing her need for the touch of another human being, that need for comfort that everyone requires sometime. As they resumed their walk, she noticed he left his arm around her instead of removing it. She sensed a subtle shift in their relationship that she couldn't quite pinpoint. Allison realized, not without chagrin, that she liked the feel of this man's steellike frame pressed against her.

At a height of nearly five feet eleven inches in heels, very few people had the ability to make Allison feel cosseted. She was quite used to being every bit as tall as most of the men she went out with. Neatly tucked into Cale Harding's side, she felt almost small and rather protected by his massive form. It was a unique experience for her to have a man stand a good half foot and more above her when she was wearing her highest heels.

They continued to stroll for some time in the unusually balmy New Hampshire night. Allison recognized she felt more comfortable with this man than she had with anyone in a long time. She supposed it sprang from their former acquaintanceship, but perhaps it was more than that, too.

Cale was a man who seemed to understand so many of the things she had had to face in her own career. He knew too well the nature of success and its pitfalls. Yet she was equally sure that his sympathy had limits. Here was a man who had started with nothing but his own talent and determination. That he should accomplish all he had set out to do despite the odds against him would hardly make him sympathize with someone who had had all the advantages and failed to do so.

Allison was feeling a little sorry for herself when she glanced up at Cale and discovered that he was studying her by the pale light cast by a nearby building. There was something in the eyes that slipped over her face feature by feature that caused her to shiver in spite of the warm summer night.

"Did you know I once wrote a story about you?" he asked, his voice rumbling in the bass register.

She was stunned for a moment by his question and its implication. And she knew Cale was closely observing her reaction.

"No, I had no idea you had written a story about me," she managed to bring out at last. Then curiosity took precedence over all the other emotions she was feeling. "What was it about?"

It was Cale's turn to hesitate. Rather unwillingly, he replied, "It was the story of a young man infatuated with a girl a little older than he was. A golden girl who represented all the things in life that were beyond his reach." He stopped speaking and stared straight ahead before dropping his gaze once more to meet hers.

Allison could scarcely believe what she was hearing. To think that this man had once actually written a story about her was mind-boggling. She would have liked to ask him so much more, but the words on the tip of her tongue refused to be voiced aloud. Even if the story were true, even if Cale had been infatuated with her all those years ago, what difference could it make to either of them now? He was certainly no longer that infatuated young man and she was no one's golden girl at the age of thirty-two.

"Did you sell the story?" she inquired, at a loss for any other comment.

That brought a slow smile to Cale's rugged features. "Yes, in fact, that story was my first big sale. *The New Yorker* paid me five hundred dollars for it while I was still in college."

"I . . . I'm glad you sold it," she said in a congratulatory tone.

"No more than I was at the time, believe me." He grinned, his expression telling her that it had been far more than the money for him. "That five hundred dollars kept me going for a long time, thanks to you in a way."

44

Cale gave her shoulder a casual squeeze as if to say he still gave her part of the credit.

"I would love to read it sometime. Do you still have a copy of it?" Allison tried her best to sound casual.

"I suppose I do somewhere," Cale answered noncommittally. "I travel around a great deal so I couldn't say for sure where it would be right now." He was obviously content to let the entire subject rest.

Allison knew then that if she ever did want to see the story, she would have to find a way of obtaining a copy on her own. For some reason she was at a loss to explain, Cale was hesitant to discuss that particular piece of his writing. She found it improbable that a man of his stature and experience could possibly find the topic embarrassing. Perhaps as an example of his earlier work, he now considered it undeserving of attention. She decided the wisest thing to do was to follow his lead and allow the subject to be dropped.

Cale twisted the wrist casually slung around her shoulders in order to see the face of his watch. "It's getting late, Allison," he said reluctantly, or at least she thought there was some reluctance in his voice. "I guess I better be getting you back to your room. Classes start bright and early in the morning for you, and I have a full day of research ahead of me," he concluded as they made a U turn and started back in the direction of the cluster of dormitories.

"It's been wonderful seeing you again, Cale," she murmured, pointing out the building that housed her room.

"I'll be here awhile longer finishing up my preliminary work. I would like to see you again," he announced, enclosing her hand in his. "Will you have dinner with me one night this week?"

"I would love to," she came back quickly, too quickly, she decided in retrospect.

While she admitted she found Cale attractive beyond anything she had imagined at the beginning of the evening, she did not want to appear too eager to be in his company. She had no illusions about the fact that a man like Cale doubtlessly had plenty of eager young women at his beck and call. She had always prided herself on being different from other women and this was going to be no exception. Allison told herself that she had no intention of becoming interested in this man. For one thing, he was famous now, and for another, she was at least four years his senior. Furthermore, she sensed some danger lurking just beneath the surface that even she was afraid to put into words.

"I know a cozy little restaurant not far from here where we could go," Cale was saying as her attention finally reverted to him.

Allison realized that he was patiently waiting for her to tell him where her room was located. Apparently, Cale had every intention of escorting her directly to her door.

"I'm on the second floor, room 232," she said as they started up the flight of stairs. "You don't have to walk me up here, you know. I'm sure I am perfectly safe on my own." She followed that statement with a rather brittle, nervous laugh.

"I'm afraid the matter of your safety never entered my mind," he said, cutting the episode down to size.

He held the hall door open for her, and she passed through, duly chastised. Allison stopped in front of the door to her room and dug about in her handbag for a moment until she came up with the key.

"Allow me." Cale swept the key from her hand without warning and slipped it into the lock. Then he opened the door and stepped back to grant her entrance.

"Thank you," Allison said as she fumbled in the dark for the light switch. She flicked it on and the rather spartan room behind her stood illuminated.

"I see your room is very much like you," observed Cale as he glanced over her shoulder. "Neat and precise and everything in order. You are a creature of habit, aren't you?"

"I don't think you have any idea what kind of creature I am," she countered, taken aback that he should find it so easy to determine her personal habits. She reminded herself that as a writer Cale had to be an astute observer of human nature, but that made her all the more wary of him as he stood in front of her like some giant sequoia. "If this were New York, I'd invite you in for a nightcap," she suggested, tossing her long blond hair over one shoulder in an unconscious gesture. "But, as you can see, my dormitory room came without the amenities."

"I'm not so sure of that." Suddenly very much the typical male, he smiled a rather intoxicating smile as his eyes lit upon the neatly made single bed.

Allison's eyes followed his and then came back to meet his gaze with a nonchalance that had taken her years to cultivate. "Scarcely enough room for one, let alone two," she commented, knowing that this time she had accurately read his mind. Cale was not the only one who knew something of human nature.

"That depends on the intention, doesn't it?" he teased,

his golden eyes shimmering in the harsh light cast by the overhead fixture.

Allison knew then that he was treating her in that same light, flirtatious way he would any attractive woman. In one sense, it was a relief to her. She would hate to be forever regarded as his former teacher. At the same time, she wasn't sure just how she did want to be regarded by this man.

"Well, as you said, it is getting late and we both have a full day tomorrow," she prompted when Cale failed to make any move to leave. This seemed to elicit no response from him either. Finally she was forced to reach out and put a hand on his arm. Although his eyes were partially closed, she knew full well he was watching every move she made. Her own studied gaze slipped from the half-closed eyes to the strong sculpted nose settling finally on the full sensuous mouth. There her glance seemed riveted, much to her dismay and wonderment. "Cale . . ." Allison's voice came out rather breathless and husky, not at all as she had meant it to sound.

Cale took a step toward her. She felt his touch on the length of hair that fell onto her shoulders. He seemed mesmerized by its softness and ran his fingers through it several times, each time more boldly than the last.

"You always did have beautiful hair, Allison," he said in a raspy voice as he released his hold and looked down into her half-puzzled, half-expectant face. "I've always wondered if it was as soft to the touch as it looked."

That was when Allison knew that Cale had every intention of kissing her. It was all part of the curiosity about the "golden girl" he had carried with him all those years.

It seemed that he would at last have the chance to satisfy that curiosity.

Allison had to admit to a certain curiosity about him as well. She found Cale a wildly attractive man, that much was true, but it was more than that. She wanted to find out for herself if that sense of danger lurking just beneath the surface was merely a figment of her imagination or something in this man. One kiss could scarcely harm either one of them. Why not give in to their natural curiosity about each other? she asked herself as she felt two strong hands span her waist and draw her even closer to the man's granite-hard chest.

"Allison . . ."

Her name came out on a breath that sent a strange quiver down her back. She allowed herself to go soft against Cale for the sake of their mutual experiment and found her own hands clasping the taut waist beneath the suit jacket he wore unbuttoned.

Then the moment of truth came as Cale lowered his head and found her mouth with unerring accuracy. His lips were soft and rough at the same instant. Allison would have liked to think about how this could be, but her full attention was required by what those very lips were doing to hers.

This was not a tentative kiss, but neither was it the passionate meeting between a man and a woman who have been lovers. Instead, it was an alternately soft and demanding expression of a man's curiosity stored up inside him too long.

From the beginning, Allison had every intention of controlling the kiss, as she had done so often in the past with other men. She would be the one to determine how far and how long this intimacy prevailed. But then she found her best intentions going astray as curiosity became secondary to the sensuality unleashed by Cale's mouth taking command of hers. Helen had been correct in her assessment. If there was any teaching to be done now, Cale would be the one to do it.

Allison was bewildered and stunned to discover that there was anything about a kiss that she did not already know. As Cale Harding was an unusual man, so was his own brand of intimacy. He seemed intent on tasting her lips and mouth and even the tip of her tongue, exploring every bit of her with a surety and leisure that left Allison feeling she had never really been kissed before.

He did not try to pry her lips apart forcibly or thrust his tongue into her mouth in an impatient display of passion as so many men would have under the circumstances, but instead took his time savoring all that she was, all that he imagined she could be.

Whether by deliberate forethought or merely by chance, Cale's patience proved to be in his favor. Allison found herself enjoying the taste and feel of his mouth as well and realized that it was an opportunity that few men afforded a woman. It was obvious Cale wanted her to discover him in the same way he wanted to discover her.

Then in those brief moments before they both sensed they would draw apart, the nature of their response changed, becoming inflamed with a passion that neither had expected nor sought. Now Cale's mouth sought hers in a way that demanded she open up to him and grant access to the dark, moist recesses. It was with eagerness that Allison did so. She wanted to be kissed by this man with an intensity she had known with no other, and he seemed determined to do just that for both their sakes.

She could not help but wonder in the back of her mind why one man's kiss could leave a woman cold while another's made her want to wrap herself around him and never let go. She was a woman, not a child, and she knew herself well enough by now to realize that she wanted this man, perhaps even more than it seemed he wanted her.

Then common sense reasserted itself, and Allison knew it was long past the time to end the experiment. Cale sensed her withdrawal before she made the slightest move and immediately followed suit. They pulled back from each other and stood there for a moment without speaking.

Allison concentrated on the third button on his shirt, unable to meet the eyes she knew she would encounter if she were to lift her head a fraction of an inch. She needed a minute or two to collect her scattered wits, and she preferred that Cale remain ignorant of the power he had wielded over her while she had been in his arms.

Self-preservation was a strong force, and that was the force that now took hold of Allison. She finally raised her eyes to meet those she sensed waited for her.

"And has your curiosity been satisfied, Cale Harding?" she inquired with what she hoped was a casual air.

He gave a little grunt that might have been a laugh. "No more or less than yours, Allison Saunders," he said with a shrug.

"I enjoyed our walk and the chance to talk with you," she went on, in full possession of her wits once more. "Thank you, Cale," she concluded, offering him her hand in a gesture that did not strike her as amusing until some time later that night.

"It was a pleasure seeing you again," he replied, striking the same note of formality she had injected into her own tone. "I'll give you a call about dinner," he added as an afterthought.

"Yes . . . well, good night, then," she said, trying to bring the evening to a close on a casual note, realizing full well that the odds were against her ever hearing from this man after tonight.

"Good night, Allison," he said with the same nonchalance.

Then Cale did an about-face and strolled down the hall toward the stairway, whistling softly under his breath.

CHAPTER THREE

The next morning Allison awoke at her usual early hour, and never having been one to lie about in bed, she quickly took her shower. She slipped her long legs into a pair of designer jeans, the most informal wear she had in her wardrobe, and donned a cerise silk blouse. A pair of backless high-heeled slings, all the rage in New York that summer, completed her outfit.

Then began the process that was second nature to her. After rolling her hair up in hot curlers, she turned on the lighted make-up mirror she had brought with her and went to work transforming the face before her. Two different shades of foundation were carefully applied after a good moisturizer and then topped off with a light matte of translucent powder. Her eyes and lips were next, receiving the same attention to detail. Finally she sat back, satisfied with what she saw reflected in the mirror.

It was the identical routine Allison went through every morning, rain or shine, whether she was going out or simply staying at home. Deeply embedded in her subconscious was the thought she must look her best at all times. It was expected of her. And she saw nothing unusual about the procedure she followed each morning with almost militarylike discipline.

With a dab of expensive French perfume to each wrist and a good, thorough brushing to her hair, she felt she was ready at last to face the day. She gathered up the notebook she intended to use for class, slung a leather handbag over her shoulder, and gave the room one last glance as she went out the door. She thought of Cale's comment last night about the preciseness of her life and realized that he was no doubt correct in his assessment.

She was a creature of habit in many ways, but then most people were. For the past few years, she had always had a time schedule that demanded she be in a specific place at a specific hour. Her long hours and full schedule required that she be organized if things were not to overwhelm her.

Allison mentally ran through her walk with Cale the evening before and the incident in her room that had followed. In the clear light of day, she decided she had definitely overreacted. After all, she had been kissed by some of the best, and he could be little different from other men in that. She did not deny that Cale had turned out to be a damned attractive specimen, but she must have been particularly vulnerable last night to imagine that he was as special as she had tried to make him out to be.

Allison tripped down the stairs and out into the sunny, brisk New Hampshire morning. The campus of Dartmouth College was one of the most picturesque she had seen. On an early summer morning, it was at its best.

She was walking along the path that led to the building where her first class was to meet when two familiar voices called out to her across the stretch of green lawn.

54

ance was still going to be a problem for her despite her diatribe to the opposite.

She had worked unflaggingly on her story, a story about the difficulties of a woman trying to find herself in a world that refused to take her seriously. The technical ability of her writing was deemed reasonably good, but that had been the single favorable comment. The class had torn apart her efforts to show that life could be difficult for someone from an advantaged background. She had found the criticism particularly hard to bear since the piece had been autobiographical.

The instructor had told them they should start by writing about what they knew best. It was an old cliché, but nevertheless true. Well, that was what Allison had done, but she had been stunned by the covert hostility and lack of sympathy from her fellow classmates. She decided part of the problem had been that her story was too easily identified with her. From the first paragraph, it had been obvious who had written the anonymous story; she had lost the objectivity of her audience right there. She vowed that next time she would make sure that her signature on the story was not so apparent.

Allison had come to the summer workshop with the express purpose of finding out if she had any real talent for writing beyond the slick advertising copy she had turned out and the nice little blurbs she had written to publicize the boutique. Now she was not sure whether she was even going to be given a fair chance to find out that much. Human behavior was human behavior, no matter what group was represented. She tried to rationalize the class's cutting remarks by telling herself that she was there to learn, and that she would never do that if everyone said nice but insincere things about her work. Perhaps after all this time she had yet to develop a thick-enough skin.

With a determination that few people realized she possessed, Allison decided then and there that she would not allow herself to be defeated. She would work twice as hard on the next assignment and make doubly sure it was still hers without giving that fact away with every word she wrote.

She sat down at the portable typewriter she had brought with her and made a half dozen false starts before giving a disgusted grunt at the sight of the growing pile of crumpled papers in the wastebasket beside the desk. Surely, after all she had lived through, she had something meaningful and interesting to say. If she didn't have that, all the technical ability in the world couldn't help her.

She thought back over her life and realized that one person stood out as an interesting character for a story—her grandmother, a woman who had lived until the age of eighty-seven and whose spirit had never failed her, not even in the end. It was with renewed vigor that Allison spent the greater part of the next two hours working and reworking the character sketch of that indomitable woman. When she had finished, she knew it was the best thing she had ever done. Yet it could be a story about anyone's grandmother. It had that universal appeal she now realized had been missing in her first story.

She was feeling much better about herself and was even able to admit that perhaps the criticism targeted at her first attempt had been justified. The class had been pretty brutal with several of the other stories as well.

She put the character sketch in her notebook and picked up the text on fiction writing. The workshop in general fiction had been assigned three chapters to read and to do an analysis for tomorrow and she had barely had a chance to start either portion. She was deep in thought when the jarring ring of the telephone at her elbow nearly sent her book crashing to the floor. She picked up the receiver and spoke into it absentmindedly, trying not to sound too surprised to hear Cale Harding's voice on the other end.

"I'm sorry I haven't called you before now, Allison." His words were apologetic, if not his tone. "I ran into a snag with my publisher and had to be out of town for a couple of days. I just got back this afternoon."

"That's all right. I've been rather busy with classes and writing assignments," she responded rather pointedly, wanting him to know that she had not been sitting around waiting for his call like some lovestruck teen-ager. The days were long past when Allison waited around for any man. She had learned that lesson some years ago and had learned it well.

"How's it going?" Cale asked, whether out of politeness or genuine interest she couldn't tell.

"I'm learning a great deal," she began obliquely. "I had my first story·crucified in class this morning, but I've managed to recover, and I have just finished what may be my best piece of writing to date."

"Give it a chance, Allison," he said in a low voice. "We both know it takes a lot more than three weeks of work-shops to make a writer."

"I'm well aware of that," she replied, trying to keep the waspishness out of her voice.

Cale must have realized he sounded a bit patronizing. "I should be telling you that of all people." His laughter was directed at himself. "I keep forgetting you taught me a great deal of what I know about writing."

"I'm not sure any great writer *learns* how to write. Oh, someone can teach you the mechanics and even tell you the correct way to construct sentences and stories, but the step between being a competent writer and a great writer has to be something that is self-taught, if at all," she said, recognizing she was the one now handing out lectures.

"Yes, Miss Saunders," he said, bringing her back down to earth with a resounding thud.

"As you said, Mr. Harding, once a teacher, always a teacher." She found some small measure of enjoyment in reminding him of his own words on that subject.

"Touché!" In that single word, he acknowledged the game of one-upmanship had been a draw. "Much as I delight in verbal parrying with a worthy opponent, what I really called about was to see if you can have dinner with me Saturday night."

Allison immediately noted that he said *can,* not *want,* when issuing the invitation and responded accordingly. "Yes, I *can* have dinner with you." Her voice was smoothly gracious, but she knew he had not failed to pick up on her choice of words.

"Would seven thirty be convenient?" This time it was a direct question.

Allison relented just a little. "Yes, seven thirty would be fine, Cale."

"I wish I could see you before Saturday," he added, somewhat to Allison's surprise. Cale Harding was not a man to show his emotions easily. She was quite sure of that. "But I'm behind on my work already. Going out on Saturday is going to be my reward."

"So, I'm to be the reward for your good behavior?" she teased.

"I didn't exactly say for good behavior," he came back just as quickly.

She could see that this man was going to be a challenge. He never missed the slightest nuance, the merest turn of a phrase. She wondered if any man or woman had gotten the best of Cale Harding.

"Well, if you don't behave yourself, I'll just have to give you a good rap on the knuckles with my ruler," she said in a deliberately prim voice she knew would raise a laugh from him. And it did.

He was still chuckling when he made his next suggestion. "I'll tell you what, Miss Saunders. I'll promise to behave if you promise to leave the dreaded ruler at home Saturday night."

"You've got yourself a deal," she said, finally allowing herself to laugh along with him. "Besides, I made up the part about the ruler."

"That's all right . . ." He continued after the briefest of pauses. "I made up the part about behaving myself."

"You always were incorrigible, Cale Harding," she said, with a click of her tongue.

"Then perhaps you'll just have to take me in hand and see what you can make of me." He chuckled again, obviously enjoying the fact that for every comeback she managed he had another. "All I have ever needed was the right woman."

Allison sensed a certain truthfulness in his last statement, but chose to treat it as she had his previous comments—with a sense of humor. "The right *woman* or the right *women*?" she said with just the right touch of lightness.

"You know what they say about safety in numbers?" he parried, knowing he had almost gone serious on her for a moment.

"In that case, perhaps I should bring along several of your adoring fans as chaperons," she suggested in an innocent voice, or as innocent as she could make it considering her outrageous suggestion.

"You wouldn't!" He breathed into the receiver so that she could actually hear the air going in and out of his lungs.

"No, of course, I wouldn't." She laughed, knowing then she had had him just for a moment. "Your reputation when it comes to your adoring public is rather well-known."

"And what about my reputation as a man?" He put it to her as part of the joke, but Allison found herself considering his question quite seriously.

"I try to judge a man for what he is, not on the basis of his reputation," she replied, thinking of the newspaper articles she had read linking his name with that woman or another. Whatever he might say to the contrary, it was obvious that Christian Trent did not always live the life of the hermit. But this wasn't Christian Trent, she reminded herself for the hundredth time. This man was Cale Harding, and as he had pointed out to her himself, they were not necessarily one and the same.

"Well, I just stopped off at the house to pick up some papers I had forgotten," Cale started to explain. Allison knew their conversation was coming to an end, and she almost hated to have that happen. She had enjoyed bantering back and forth with him. She supposed it was easier to talk with Cale over the telephone when she wasn't reminded every moment of his imposing physical appearance. He could be an overpowering figure in person. He was somewhat less intimidating as a disembodied voice. "I have to get back to the library and finish up for the day, otherwise I won't deserve to take the night off with you," he said in conclusion.

Allison somehow wished he had said *evening* instead of *night*. There was a connotation to the word *night* when Cale said it. "Yes . . ." she agreed in a slightly mollified tone. "And I still have hours of work to do before tomorrow's classes."

"Then in case I don't have the chance to talk to you again before the weekend, I'll pick you up Saturday night at seven thirty, room 232." Cale repeated the information as if he were jotting it down in some little black book he carried with him.

"I'll see you on Saturday then," Allison repeated, knowing she would remember without writing down a word.

"Take care, golden girl," he said, close to the receiver.

"Good-bye, Cale," she murmured thoughtfully as she hung up the telephone.

Allison stood there for a minute or two, staring at the telephone but not seeing it. Was that the impetus behind his invitation for dinner? Was he still caught up in a decade-old dream about a young woman he had once known? If he was, she had a sinking feeling that Cale was going to be gravely disappointed when he discovered that dreams were always better than reality. That anticipation was more exciting than experience.

He had warned her that Cale Harding and his alter ego, Christian Trent, were not the same man. Well, she could say the same to him. The girl she had been at twenty-two was not the woman she was at thirty-two.

Then she stood in the middle of her dormitory room and laughed aloud at herself. She was worried about Cale! If there was anyone who deserved her concern it was herself. He was a dangerous man for her in more ways than she could count. Just being with him made her feel a little like that girl again, and that in itself was unwise. She was too old to have her feet leave the ground again. She had had them firmly planted on old terra firma for a good while now, and she was not about to allow that to change. Allison had seen too much of reality to believe in the fantasy of love.

As Allison dressed that Saturday night, she seemed to deliberately choose an outfit and a hairstyle that emphasized her maturity and sophistication rather than the youthfulness she still possessed in great abundance. It was almost as if she wanted to make the point that she was no longer a girl, no longer a "golden girl."

For the second time that day she applied her usual sophisticated make-up. Then she swept her hair up in a style that accentèd her high cheekbones and large topaz-colored eyes. The dress she chose was simply cut and without adornment, but styled for the tall figure on the thin side. It was another silk in powder blue with short capped sleeves and a narrow skirt. She added a leather handbag and shoes in the same shade of blue. A touch of silver in her ears and at her wrist in a finely wrought pair of earrings and matching bracelet completed her ensemble. She took a final look at herself in the inadequate mirror provided in her room and put the matter of her appearance totally out of her mind for the rest of the evening.

It was not personal vanity that drove Allison to look her best always. It was more a matter of habit. She was not a woman to primp. Once she had done the "window dressing," she promptly dismissed the subject from her mind.

She was dressed and waiting when the knock came at her door at precisely seven thirty. It seemed as though Cale was also a believer in punctuality.

Allison opened the door and there he stood—all six feet four inches of him—dressed in a beautifully tooled leather jacket that appeared to have been worked to the softness of a fawn. The golden leather only served to emphasize the gold flecks she now recognized as a regular feature in his eyes. He wore a darker shade of brown trousers, which hugged the lean hips as if they had been tailored to them. In retrospect, Allison realized that a man of his size no doubt had every stitch of clothing he wore specially made for him. Just as she, with her height, slender figure, and plentiful pocketbook, had nearly all of her things designed for her.

"Hello, Cale." She tried to sound nonchalant as she gave him a welcoming smile, but suddenly she was a bundle of nerves. She couldn't remember the last time she had had butterflies, but they were definitely there now.

"You look very lovely this evening, Allison," he responded with the expected compliment. Only in this case, the compliment was genuine. She did look lovely, indeed.

"You're right on time," she observed.

"I wouldn't want to get any black marks for being

tardy, now would I?" he said with a chuckle lodged in the back of his throat. "I see you're ready to go." It was a statement rather than the customary rhetorical question.

"Yes." Allison gave him one of her rare Mona Lisa smiles. She picked up her handbag from the bed and walked past him out the door.

She tried not to show her surprise when Cale indicated that the tan-and-brown Bronco in the parking lot was his. She was learning not to expect the expected of this man. Allison would have thought he could well afford a fancy sports car, but apparently his taste did not run to fancy cars. If she had thought about it longer, she might have reasoned for herself that a man who traveled a great deal and hauled a large typewriter and reams of material might well opt for a small truck rather than a car that was all show.

"I've been staying in the New Hampshire mountains the past several weeks." Cale seemingly read her mind and began to explain the reason behind his choice of transportation. "In fact, I expect to be up in the mountains most of the fall and winter. A four-wheel drive is the only practical mode of transportation."

She gave him an enigmatic smile, as if to say "Did she ask?" and allowed him to settle her in the passenger side. It was rough going in her narrow skirt, but she managed with his help. As it turned out, Cale practically lifted her off the ground and into the Bronco. Allison was once more amazed by his sheer physical strength. She could feel the muscles beneath his jacket straining against the material as he placed her in the front seat.

"How did your research go the rest of the week?" Allison inquired as she smoothed the skirt of her dress and laid her handbag across her lap.

Cale took one easy step into the driver's seat. He turned to answer as he switched the ignition on and backed out of the parking space. "If you're asking if I deserve to take the night off, then the answer is a definite yes. I think I got more done in the past couple of days than I usually do in a week. Some of your good influence must be rubbing off on me," he said, lifting one expressive eyebrow in her direction before he concentrated on the road ahead.

Cale drove off the campus and headed through the town of Hanover, making small talk as they went. Allison found herself content to take in the scenery of the New Hampshire countryside in the failing light of the evening. It was all lush and muted and still; she could well understand why so many artists sought out this place to work. It both inspired and pacified the soul, its natural, untouched beauty a sort of tranquilizer.

Neither spoke of the incident that had taken place between them the weekend before. Yet there was a heightened awareness between them that neither could deny. Allison found her gaze slipping along the long muscular leg nearest to her. Everything about Cale seemed to be big and muscular and larger than life. Realizing the direction in which her own thoughts were leading her, she quickly averted her eyes and stared out the window.

She must not allow her imagination to run away with her. She and Cale scarcely knew each other, and in a case like that Allison felt that slow and easy was always the best policy. She had been involved in too many whirlwind romances in her life to wish to enter into another at this stage of the game.

"I think you'll enjoy this place," Cale was saying in reference to the mock-pub restaurant he had been describing to her. "Of course, it's hardly the kind of restaurant you would frequent in New York, but it has a lot of local color and the food is excellent."

"I'm sure I'll enjoy it. If I wanted everything to be like New York, I would have stayed in New York," she said with a touch of reproach. "I suddenly realized when I was getting ready to come to New Hampshire for the workshop that while I have seen most of the great cities of this country and Europe, I haven't ever really gotten out into the countryside of any of the places I've been. I have always thought of myself as the cosmopolitan type, but I'm beginning to see it might be more a matter of never having tried anything else."

"I love the city if I want to see a good play or take in an exhibition, but I've learned in the past five years that I work better when I'm in the country." Cale picked up the conversation and applied it to himself. "We're almost there now," he added, spotting some landmark in the distance.

In several minutes, he pulled off the highway and into the parking lot in front of a large rustic building that discreetly displayed the name *Murphy's Pub* above the porch door. Cale repeated the same procedure getting her out of the Bronco as he had earlier getting her into it. Allison took a moment to regain her land legs, and then they proceeded inside.

Allison felt as though she were entering a world quite foreign to her. Murphy's Pub was a fairly informal place with open beamed ceilings and roughhewn log walls. Bare floors were covered here and there with old-fashioned rugs, which she surmised were braided from rags. She had once seen something similar in an antique shop on one of New York's avenues.

There was a mammoth stone fireplace at one end of the large room, with what she supposed were fake logs burning merrily away. No doubt in the winter months these were replaced with the real thing. There was a carved wooden bar off to one side, and in between were a dozen or more tables set for dining. The atmosphere was subdued, but Cale informed her that when the college was in regular session, the level of noise on a late weekend night was considerably higher than at present.

Allison had never been one not to try something new, though she had not always made a special effort to do so. Yet she found the atmosphere of the place congruous with the mental image she had of Cale. In his own way, he, too, was large and rustic.

A hostess greeted them inside the front door, dressed in some kind of pseudo-Western wear. Apparently, one did not have to live in Arizona to be a cowboy these days. Allison was only too cognizant of the look the woman gave Cale before she escorted them to a table by the fireplace. Apparently, without requesting the best table in the house Cale had been given just that. From their vantage point, they had a full view of the entire room, but there was a feeling of privacy too.

Cale drew out Allison's chair and had her comfortably seated before he moved to the place opposite her and took his own seat. As he scooted his chair closer, their knees collided abruptly under the table.

"Excuse me, Allison." He laughed a little as he shifted in his seat to accommodate his long legs. "These places

71

obviously weren't built for a man or a woman with any legs to them."

"It's something I run into all the time," she reassured him. "I even have to sit sideways in the desks they have in the classrooms at Dartmouth. You would think with the average American supposedly getting taller with each generation, they would do something about it. But I do find more advantages than disadvantages to being tall."

Cale studied her for a moment with a strange light in his eyes. "You know, I never thought of you as being particularly tall."

Allison felt her face grow warm under his less-than-subtle scrutiny. "I'm five feet eight without my heels—reasonably taller than most of the women I know." She gave him the once-over before posing her own question. "I don't suppose many people do seem tall to a man of your stature. How tall are you, anyway?"

Cale frowned for a moment, not unhappily, but with a touch of theatrics she found amusing. "I was six four the last time anyone measured me. I haven't had any reason to check that in a good many years, however."

At least she had been right on that one point, Allison thought with satisfaction. Then someone put a coin in the jukebox. The lamenting strains of a country-and-western song came drifting across the room toward them. She must have appeared startled by the choice of music for Cale picked up on it immediately.

"Not the type of music you usually listen to?" he inquired with an innocent expression that made Allison wonder what he was up to.

Was bringing her here tonight some type of test? Was he trying to see how she would react under circumstances he felt were far different than those she usually encountered? Her world had not been as insulated as he seemed to think.

"Oh, I wouldn't say that," she murmured, taking a sip of ice water from the glass in front of her. "I think Crystal Gayle's music transcends the strict lines of country-and-western and popular, don't you?"

Allison knew that had surprised him. He had not expected her to recognize the song or the singer. Well, she had shown him! It was a bit of luck, however, that she had heard the young woman perform that song on television not too long ago.

Cale gave her a surreptitious glance under the guise of studying his menu. She had to smile in the knowledge that she had pulled that one off rather well. Allison had expected this to be a simple dinner date, not some kind of testing ground.

"I've only eaten here twice," Cale finally informed her, looking up. "But I can recommend the Alaskan king crab or the New York strip. Both were good when I ordered them."

At the mere thought of eating a large dinner, Allison began to feel full. She just wasn't used to eating large quantities of anything. When the waitress arrived to take their order, she made a point of requesting a small portion of steak, done very rare. "I'll have a small salad with that and the asparagus," concluded Allison, closing the menu.

Cale gave her an incredulous look. "I'll have the large order of crab legs, baked potato, salad, and the asparagus," he said, seeming to miss the fact that the young waitress hung on his every word. "We would like a drink before our dinner and a bottle of chilled light burgundy with our meal," he instructed, looking up at the girl and bestowing one of his most seductive smiles on her.

The girl literally beamed back at him and promised to send the cocktail waitress to their table immediately.

"Shame on you, Cale Harding." Allison chastised him with a crooked smile.

"I know . . ." He grinned wolfishly. "But I always get such excellent service that way." There was no false modesty in that claim. Allison was sure he did. "Now, what would you like to drink?" Cale asked as the cocktail waitress scurried toward their table.

CHAPTER FOUR

"I . . . I think I'll have a Scotch and water, light on the Scotch, please," Allison told the cocktail waitress when the girl was able to tear her eyes away from Cale.

"Make that a Chivas and water for the lady, and I'll have a Chivas on the rocks," Cale cut in smoothly, his manner impeccable. Allison had no cause to object to his display of highhandedness.

"You always have to have the last word, don't you, Cale?" she said, after the perky young waitress had walked away, her hips swaying beneath the short cowgirl skirt.

"It has been my experience that if you don't order Scotch by name, you never know what you're getting," he said, deftly sidestepping the issue. "You have to know what you want, Allison, before you can ever get it."

"And you've always known that, haven't you?" she said sardonically, but with far more truth than she realized.

"Not always." He smiled laconically. "But I have known what I *don't* want, and that simple fact has made a difference in my personal life and in my career."

Something in the way Cale spoke made Allison feel that she could never be as old as this man. She wondered what it was that had made him that way.

"Why don't you tell me what happened to you after college?" she suggested, once they had their drinks. "I still don't know how Cale Harding became Christian Trent."

"Well, as I told you before, I sold that story to *The New Yorker* while I was still in school. I'd also been working on a novel off and on the whole time I was at Yale. I showed it to a few of the right people evidently, because once I was graduated one of the major publishing houses showed an interest in it and advanced me enough money to live on for the next six months while I polished the final draft. As it turned out, that first novel became something of a best seller much to everyone's surprise, including mine."

"That wasn't *Journey,* was it?" she asked incredulously, referring to the first novel she had ever read of Christian Trent's. It had become something of a cult book.

"Yes, as a matter of fact, it was," he replied, apparently surprised that she had known about that early work.

"I thought it was marvelous!" Allison exclaimed. "I always admired the courage of that boy hitchhiking across the country by himself. *Journey* has some of the best character studies I think I've ever read. Where did you get the idea for that book?" she asked out of genuine interest, both as a reader and as a writer.

"It was simple, really," Cale said, not altogether serious. "I ran away from home when I was fifteen and hitched a ride with whoever would pick me up. Even then I was smart enough to keep a journal."

"You mean to tell me that all those experiences that boy went through actually happened to you?" Allison was stunned, remembering some of the terrifying episodes in the book.

"Let's just say that the journal I kept provided a basis for the novel," Cale replied evasively.

If that were half true, she was beginning to understand why Cale seemed older than his years. Little wonder he sometimes had a certain agelessness to his personality. He had been out on his own before she had even been allowed to date. She might be four years older than he according to the calendar, but when it came to experience he won hands down. And not all of it had been pleasant, by any means.

"*Journey* was the most autobiographical of my books, but I did enhance some of the scenes to make my point," he sought to reassure her.

"What happened then?" Allison needed to know.

"I thought you said you read the book," Cale came back, with a look of simulated surprise on his face.

"I did read the book. I meant what happened to you," she repeated, gazing up into his eyes and forgetting everything else for a moment. "What happened to Cale Harding?"

"Well, the police finally matched me up with the description that my grandmother had put out on me, and they shipped me home," he said unemotionally.

"Your mother must have been worried sick," Allison interjected in a soft voice.

A strange expression flickered across Cale's face before he finally chose to answer. "My mother could not have cared less if I came home or not," he stated without preamble. At the look of disbelief on her face, he went on, "You cannot judge everyone else by what your family would have done, Allison."

"But surely your parents—"

"My father was killed in a factory accident when I was eleven," he said harshly. "My mother cared about one person and that was herself. I don't blame the woman, she was ill-equipped to be anyone's mother and I was not an easy child to handle. We never did get along, Allison. It was better for both of us that I ran away."

She took a good long swallow of her Scotch and water before she dared to speak again, and even then she was half afraid to say it. "I imagine your mother is very proud of you now."

"My mother has no idea that her son is Christian Trent, as far as I know," Cale said. He continued when he saw that she still did not understand. "I thought it was common knowledge at Park Academy at the time. My mother ran off with a man when I was a senior in high school. I haven't seen or heard from her since."

"I . . . I'm sorry, Cale. . . . I had no idea. I wouldn't have brought it up if I had known it was going to be such a painful subject for you." Allison felt hot tears gather in the corners of her eyes and bowed her head to hide their appearance from him.

"Don't cry for me, honey," he said, reaching out and raising her chin so that she was forced to meet his gaze. He spoke in the softest tone she had ever heard from him. "I worked out the pain a long time ago. I have no regrets now, at least not most of the time. I can't say there haven't been times when I wished my childhood had been more normal, but I've learned to accept what I can't change. In a way, I'm grateful. I believe what I came from helped me to become what I am today. I even believe I can write because of it."

Allison brushed away the stray tears and forced herself

to breathe normally. "You mean you actually believe all the disadvantages you grew up with are part of what has made you a writer?"

"I think it made me try harder, whatever I eventually decided to do. I knew early in my life that there was only one person I could rely on and that was myself. It makes you grow up, Allison. I knew if I was going to make something of myself, I was the one who had to do it. That's not a bad lesson for anyone to learn."

"Yes, I see," she said, blinking away the moisture that had gathered on the tips of her eyelashes. "Perhaps that ability you seem to have to touch the universal cord in all of us, perhaps that talent to make us laugh when we might cry, exists because you've been there and you know it firsthand. You have actually lived what most of us can only imagine."

"Don't make me out to be some kind of hero, Allison, or even worse, a martyr," Cale said, his mouth in a thin, hard line. "I'm not the only one who came up the hard way, and I've been a lot luckier than most. I've enjoyed my success, and I live exactly the way I want to now. There aren't too many people who can say that."

"I suppose you're right," she said thoughtfully, trying to put what he had told her into perspective.

"Besides—" Cale looked at her and broke into a wicked grin. "I don't usually take my dates to dinner and then regale them with stories that have them crying over the first drink. I normally wait until at least dessert before I do that."

But Allison knew that the glimpse she had been given into his private life was one he rarely if ever shared with anyone. Cale would be the last person interested in eliciting sympathy from any man or woman. She could only surmise that he had felt comfortable with her and perhaps said more than he had intended. One thing had led to another until the story had come out. She was quite sure it had not been intentional.

"Well, considering what one drink did to loosen your tongue, I can't wait to see what a second drink produces," she teased, knowing the time was right to put their earlier conversation behind them.

"Oh, no, you don't!" Cale laughed. "You'll get no more true confessions out of me tonight. If anyone is going to spill their guts, it will have to be you." Cale inclined his head toward her and looked at her appraisingly. "Or doesn't the lady have guts?"

"Oh, she has them, or at least she's learning to develop some fast," Allison retorted, flinging up her chin. "She would have to just to go out with you, Mr. Harding."

"Why, Miss Saunders, whatever do you mean?" he said, biting the corners of his mouth against a smile.

Thank God, she was saved from having to make further comment by the timely arrival of their dinner. Allison found herself giving the young waitress a grateful smile out of all proportion to her services. Cale was soon intent upon making general small talk over their steak and crab. He had known full well the insinuation behind her comment. It did take a woman with guts to take on a man like Cale Harding. He was no man for the weak or faintheart-ed.

Allison was so engrossed in her meal and especially in her conversation with Cale that she was surprised to discover some time later that she had consumed her entire dinner and helped him polish off a whole bottle of wine

80

without once being aware that Murphy's Pub had filled with people. Relaxed and feeling very much at ease, she watched with interest as a four-piece band set up their equipment on a small, makeshift stage. A dance floor miraculously appeared halfway between their table and the bar at the other end of the room.

"I assume we are about to be serenaded." Her laugh was born of pleasure and wine.

"It would appear so," Cale replied, taking a sip of his coffee.

Allison continued to watch as the band went through the motions of tuning their instruments. Then they began to play—with more enthusiasm than actual talent, in her opinion. Their repertoire seemed to consist of standard country-and-western fare as well as some of the current popular hits. When the band changed pace and began to play a ballad, the dance floor filled with couples of all ages. Allison could not help but wonder what it would be like to dance with a man like Cale, but perhaps dancing was one of those social graces he had never had the time or opportunity to develop.

"Would you like to dance, Allison?" he asked, as if he had read her mind. He did seem to have a maddening tendency to do that. "I'm no Fred Astaire, but I promise to trample only on my own feet."

"I would love to dance, and I'm no Ginger Rogers," she quipped as she allowed him to escort her to the dance floor.

Allison had forgotten just how tall Cale really was until he took her in his arms. She enjoyed the rare experience of resting her head against a man's chin instead of looking him straight in the eyes, or worse, looking down at the top of his head.

The band seemed to recognize they had a good thing going and followed the ballad with another slow number. Allison thought the lights in the restaurant purposely dimmed to add to the atmosphere, but perhaps she was imagining things.

She discovered that for a man his size Cale was a very graceful dancer. She was able to follow his lead with comparative ease as he guided her around the floor. The dance area was getting more crowded by the minute, and whether of necessity or simply because he wanted to, Cale pulled her even closer to him until Allison could feel the outline of his body imprinted along the length of hers.

His hands moved with maddening slowness down her back to span her waist, half-embracing the curve of her hips in the process. She could feel their warmth penetrate the silky material of her dress and wondered if their heat had somehow permanently branded her flesh beneath.

She looked about her and saw that most of the other couples were dancing in much the same manner. She lost her self-consciousness about entwining her hands behind his neck. Her action brought them into even closer contact; very little was left to the imagination. Her breasts were flattened against Cale's chest, her hips fitted to the curve of his, and their legs half entwined as they swayed back and forth in a simulation of far more than dancing.

Cale's breath was like a hot tropical breeze stirring the wisps of hair about her face. His scent was a heady combination of wine and coffee and after shave, quite intoxicating in its own right. Allison had no idea that her own sweet mixture of wine and exotic perfume was even more inflaming.

They moved together as one, as if they had been dancing together far longer than a matter of mere minutes, their inner rhythms matching step for step. She felt Cale's hand leave her waist and caressingly make its way up the small of her back. It lingered for a moment before continuing on around to her ribs. His thumb was pressing the side of her breast, but he made no further move to touch her, leaving it there as some kind of erotic reminder.

Her own fingers found the soft bristles of hair at his nape, exploring the thick texture of his hair and the way it brushed the top of his shirt collar. The muscles of his neck seemed taut, as if he were wound as tightly as a spring. It was obvious to both of them that they were discovering those first intimate details about each other in the safety of a crowded room. There the limits were clearly set.

Then Cale brushed his lips across her forehead like a star blazing across the night sky, leaving a trail of white heat in its wake. In that moment, Allison found herself more aware of him than she could ever remember being aware of anyone in her life. It was as though he were making love to her right there and then. She felt her body move into his, seeking some form of satisfaction she was loath to name.

"I like the way you move, the way you feel, the way you smell," he whispered as he bent slightly and caught the tip of one ear lobe in his teeth and gave a gentle tug. His breath washed over her skin like the touch of hot coals. Yet she shivered as though she felt a sudden chill.

"Cale—" She meant to voice some protest, knowing he

was using the crowded dance floor to do as he willed, but her voice sounded altogether different. When he raised his head to gaze down into her eyes, Allison knew that what he saw there was the same desire she saw reflected in his own.

Just as Cale mouthed her name, his lips so near to hers, the slow pace of the music abruptly changed to a fast upbeat tempo that shattered the mood of intimacy.

"Would you like another cup of coffee or an after-dinner drink?" he inquired without enthusiasm as they returned to their table.

Allison sensed somehow that he wanted her to refuse and heard herself do just that in the next breath. "No. Thank you, anyway. I believe I've had enough."

They rose to their feet in unison. While Cale saw to the bill, she took a moment to detour to the ladies' room. When she came out, he was waiting—rather impatiently, it seemed to her—and he wasted no time in bundling her back into the Bronco. Allison wondered if this signaled the end of their evening. It was relatively early.

Cale appeared to be almost angry with her, a deep scowl cutting across his features as he rammed the Bronco into gear and pulled away from Murphy's Pub. What did two respectable adults do for entertainment when there was no concert or play or after-hours spot? Allison wondered as she stared straight ahead of her into the black curtain of night.

She had her answer a quarter of an hour later when Cale pulled into the driveway of a modest ranch-style house near the campus. "I'm using one of the professor's homes while he's on summer vacation with his family. I thought it might be nicer to have an after-dinner drink here than at the restaurant," he explained, helping her down from the vehicle.

It was a nice enough house, but Allison spent little time examining it in detail. She realized it would yield few clues to the man at her side as his own home might have. She vaguely noted the arrangement of the rooms as Cale indicated the doorway of what she surmised was the living room.

He sauntered over to a bar in one corner of the room and turned back to her. "Please make yourself at home. Would you care to join me in a brandy?" he inquired urbanely.

"Yes, please," she responded with the same degree of politeness, taking a seat on the crushed-velour sofa in front of the unlit fireplace. Allison told herself there was no earthly reason to be nervous, but she was nonetheless.

She reminded herself of that fact again when the soft strains of what she thought was Debussy filled the living room. Then Cale was at her side with a snifter of brandy in each hand. He gave her one and sat down on the sofa beside her, stretching his long legs out in front of him as though they had been cramped all evening.

"To old friendships . . . and new," he toasted, touching his glass to hers and taking a drink of the golden liquid, his eyes never leaving her face.

"To old friends . . ." Allison repeated, deliberately omitting the end of his toast. She was not altogether certain of what the *new* referred to, and until she did she had no wish to toast it. It was childish on her part, perhaps, but caution was one quality she had had plenty of reason to develop in recent years. She knew only too well where impulsiveness got her. She had been there often enough.

"Tell me, Allison," Cale said, moving a little closer, as if the small space between them was still too much for him. "What are your plans once the writers' workshop here is over?" The muscular thigh pressing into hers made any reasonable answer fly out of her mind.

"I . . . I'm not sure what I'll be doing for the rest of the summer," she managed to get out. "I suppose I will go back to New York and devote the next several months to writing. I have promised myself I'll have that chance at last. What will you do?" she asked, simply to have something to say so that he would have to do the talking. She was finding the atmosphere in the room stifling and couldn't seem to keep a clear head.

"Hell, I'm always doing the same thing," Cale replied, setting his brandy down on the coffee table at their feet. "I am either researching a book, writing a book, or thinking about the next one. It's an endless cycle from which I seem unable to escape."

"Do you want to?" murmured Allison, trying to ignore the hand caressing the back of her neck.

He looked at her with unreadable eyes. "Do I want to what?"

"Do you want to escape the cycle of researching and writing?" she prompted.

"I do tonight," Cale said after a brief pause. "I want to spend this night without once thinking about my work." His voice moved on quietly and slowly. "I want to spend this night with a beautiful woman in my arms."

Allison visibly stiffened. "Will any beautiful woman do, or did you have someone specific in mind?" Her voice was wintry cool, failing to conceal her sudden displeasure.

"You know there's only one woman I want in my

arms," Cale muttered in a husky tone as he moved to her side and forced her to relinquish the glass of brandy she held in her hands. He placed it on the coffee table next to his own, then resumed where he had left off.

"I don't think this is wise, Cale," she said pedantically, but she made no move to extricate herself from his embrace.

"And do you always do only what's wise, Allison?" Cale said with a faint cynical smile. "I know something happens to me when I hold you in my arms, and I think it happens for you as well. That may not be wise, but dammit, it happens to be true!" Cale rasped as his mouth sought effectively to silence hers.

His kiss was a study in self-restraint, but she could sense the passion building beneath the surface, a passion that would soon break free if she did not pull back now. She thought to, she meant to, but the intoxicating feel of Cale's mouth on hers made her lightheaded, made it impossible for a single coherent thought to form and then stay in her mind.

It was a long, shattering kiss that laid to rest forever any doubts she might have as to his effect upon her. They both knew this was what they had been waiting for all evening. The time spent in each other's arms dancing had been no more than a prelude to this moment.

Allison found herself kissing him back without reserve, her mouth móving beneath his, hot and eager for the excitement only Cale could give her. She was no child. She realized they were playing with fire and that someone would undoubtedly get burned in the process. Cale had intimated that she thought too much. Perhaps he was right. Perhaps it was time simply to feel.

She wanted desperately to forget everything and everyone but this man and the bittersweet ache he aroused in her with his kiss and the merest touch. His arms were like bands of steel around her. His kiss was as hard and hungry as if he wanted to draw even the breath of life from her lungs. His tongue furiously invaded the moist recesses of her mouth in an imitation of that more intimate act of lovemaking. She felt as though he were devouring her, that she would surely melt into his bones and become one with him.

If this was what Cale could do to her with his kiss, what would happen if he sought to do more? How could she pull back and preserve her own identity if he wanted more of her? She was nearly lost to herself now.

Sensing perhaps that she was thinking again, Cale redoubled his efforts to distract her. With his mouth still on hers, he gathered Allison up as if she weighed no more than a child and settled her across his lap. His large hands grasped her by the waist as he lifted his head for a moment to gaze into her face. Desire was clearly written on his features.

Cale wanted her. Allison was suddenly quite sure of that fact. And she wanted him as well. Cradled across his body, she suddenly felt very vulnerable, at the mercy of a man who doubtlessly could crush her with his very hands. The sheer physical reality of Cale Harding was almost frightening. If he lost control, Allison was not sure she would have the strength to stop him. A small voice in the back of her head reminded her that she would first have to *want* to stop him.

Then Cale seemed to soften toward her and his mouth began to tease and cajole hers into a response. It was as though he did not want to frighten her away with the force of his own driving need. His hands reached out to stroke her hair, wreaking havoc with her once immaculate hairdo. He drew his fingers through the loosened strands, luxuriating in its softness as it fell across his palm like a spray of gold. He bent and pressed his lips to her hair, breathing in the scent of her as though she were a fresh spring day that somehow revitalized him and gave him sustenance.

His hands caressed her shoulders and moved along the bones and muscles of her neck and upper chest with infuriating slowmotion. It seemed he intended to discover every inch of her, every secret she possessed. His teeth nibbled on the lobe of her ear and the tender skin at the base of her throat, eliciting a succession of small whimpers from her that spoke louder than any words. His hands found the row of tiny buttons down the front of her dress. With casual attention to detail, Cale touched first her eyes, then the tip of her nose, and finally her mouth. Soft, biting kisses accompanied each button he undid.

With his task nearly completed, Cale covered one silk-covered breast with a sinewy hand. He laid his mouth on the skin he had bared in his wanderings. His lips were hot to the touch, but gentle in their exploration as he trailed a string of searing kisses along her flesh.

He moved slowly, easily, so as not to startle her into bolting from his embrace, making no demands beyond allowing him to touch and caress her. Allison found herself being lulled into a sense of security, of trust. Her breath drew in sharply when he at last chose to push the material of her dress aside to grant him further access, but his approach was more worshipful than passionate.

Allison let her head fall back on Cale's shoulder and closed her eyes, concentrating on the exquisite feel of his hands on her skin. He shaped her to his will, clearly enjoying the feel of her. After caressing each breast in turn, his hands moved to her shoulders. His mouth once more sought hers. Allison's breath started to come hard and fast as she began to respond to his growing urgency.

She scarcely noticed when he slipped the dress from her shoulders and let it fall to her waist. Cale raised his head, his eyes dark and disturbed. He held her gaze with his own. He unhooked the single fastening at the front of her lacy bra, and a moment later her breasts fell freely into his hands.

He traced an erotic pattern with his finger from one pink nipple across the expanse of white skin to the other. Allison's breath caught in the back of her throat as he nipped each bud between his finger and thumb, giving a gentle but sharp tug before moving on to the other.

"Cale." She finally uttered his name a little impatiently and reached out to begin the same process with the row of buttons down the front of his shirt. Her hands were trembling. The small white buttons of his dress shirt seemed to refuse to cooperate.

Cale pulled back from her and set her down on the sofa. He gracefully got to his feet and removed his jacket and tie with precise and unhurried movements. It was as though there was no need to hurry this time of discovery, as though part of the enjoyment was savoring each and every moment of it.

He came back to her with the same unhurried attitude and gathered her once again in his arms. "You're a beautiful woman, Allison, and you have a beautiful body," he murmured in a husky voice as he lay her back on the sofa and stretched out beside her.

She gazed up at the man posed half above her, and taking courage in hand she continued to undo the buttons on his shirt. Then she pulled the material loose from the waistband of his trousers and took a moment to enjoy the sight of his bared muscles and skin.

Allison ran her fingers up the wall of his chest and rotated them in small circles, stopping to touch first one masculine equivalent to her own nipples and then the other. She watched with fascination as they, too, curled up into small erect mountains against his flesh.

His skin was surprisingly smooth and taut as it stretched across the muscles of his chest and arms. Allison helped him shrug off the shirt altogether, and then they came to each other, bare skin pressed to bare skin. The curl of hairs that ran riot down his torso brushed against her flesh, sensitizing it, making it tingle with every touch.

Cale's mouth was like a drug. She caught him to her and ran her tongue along his lower lip and then the upper, taking small nibbles, tasting him for herself. He groaned when she penetrated his mouth with her own darting tongue, flicking in and out, escaping each attempt he made to capture it with his own.

Cale's hands did not remain idle long. He found the smooth stretch of ivory skin that led to her abdomen. He lowered his head and followed the trail with his lips until he came full circle. He caught the tip of one breast in his mouth and played with it until Allison moaned her need. He nipped and licked and rolled his tongue around the ripe nipple until she unconsciously arched her back, driving her breast even deeper into his mouth. He went from one to the other and repeated the erotic process as though he would never tire of it.

"Cale!" His name passed her lips as a low groaning sign of her need. "Cale!" It was repeated with greater urgency.

"Do you want me, Allison?" he muttered against her breast.

"Yes, damn you, Cale Harding! I want you!" she admitted, out of breath, knowing his male ego had been satisfied by her admission.

"And I want you," he said huskily, taking her mouth for his own. Cale ran his hand down her thigh and moved up under her skirt, caressing the long bare length of her leg. "I've wanted you for a long time, golden girl, and now you will be mine. But I won't make you wait half as long for me as I've waited for you," he mumbled in the heat of his unleashed passion.

At his words, Allison felt a strange chill settle over her. Cale was making love to that same golden girl he had once been infatuated with, not Allison Saunders, a mature woman of thirty-two who should have known better than to get herself in this predicament. Would the past never leave her in peace? Why couldn't Cale have wanted her for the woman she was now, not the girl of ten long years ago?

It took several minutes for her lack of response to register. He stopped and looked down into her face, realizing he had lost her somewhere.

"What's wrong?" He gritted his teeth, not wanting to ask that question, sensing he would not like the answer.

"Let me go, Cale," Allison said through numb lips as

she pushed against the stone wall of his chest. "Just let me go!"

"I'll let you go just as soon as you tell me what's wrong," he said in a belligerent tone.

Allison attempted to pull her clothes around her body and cover the nakedness that now seemed like an affront to her dignity. "I don't want you," she said resentfully.

"What the hell do you mean you don't want me?" he demanded, coloring angrily. "You damned well wanted me a minute ago, lady! Do you know what men call a woman like you?" he spat out with the full force of his fury.

"I am not a tease!" she stated with more bravado than she felt caught beneath his tremendous weight. "I will not make love with you, Cale. You don't want me, Allison Saunders, age thirty-two. You want some"—she tried to gesture with her hands and found Cale had them pinned to her side—"some image of a girl you remember from a long time ago. Well, I am not that girl now. I may never have been that girl. Now, let me go."

This time he complied and released her, knowing that the intimacy between them had been rendered beyond any attempt at repair.

"Maybe you're right," he muttered, sitting up on the edge of the sofa and running distraught hands through the shock of chestnut hair. "Maybe I did start out making love to that girl, but it was you, the woman, I wanted in the end."

Free from the restraint of his arms at last, Allison sat up and tried to put herself to rights. God! She must look an absolute sight, she thought hysterically. Her clothes in disarray, her hair a mass of tangles, half up and half down.

What was she thinking of, anyway? She was too old to go in for petting on a sofa with any man.

She would be at Dartmouth for a grand total of two more weeks, and Cale—she didn't know if he would be here even that long. What had possessed her to come here with him tonight and behave as she had? She was woman enough to realize where they were headed. She did not want to have a two-week affair with any man, particularly not this man. For once she had become a part of him, how could she ever be whole on her own again?

"I . . . I would like to go back to the dorm," Allison said in the same thin tone, standing and slipping her feet into shoes that had mysteriously come off in their lovemaking. "I would like to go now."

"Allison . . ." Cale stood up and turned to her, his eyes clouded with some inexplicable emotion she interpreted to be merely disappointment. "Allison, I'm sorry, but it doesn't have to end like this. Maybe I went too fast, but dammit, woman, I've wanted you since the first moment I laid eyes on you last weekend. We could start over, take things slow and easy this time."

She knew he was trying to believe what he was saying, but she didn't think there was any slow and easy possible between them. If she saw him again, the same thing would doubtlessly happen. He wanted her, and in her weakness, she wanted him as well. There would be no halfway measures for them, of that she was certain.

"I don't think so, Cale," she said, shaking her head with vehemence. "I'm not interested in having a two-week affair with you, and we both know that's exactly where we're headed unless we end it now. I admit I want you—"

she swallowed "—but casual affairs have never been my style and I won't start now."

Cale speared her with a long stare. Then he turned his back to her and picked up the leather jacket crumpled in a heap on the floor. Without a word, he buttoned up his shirt and slipped his arms into the jacket sleeves. He ran his hand through his hair, this time in a conscious effort to straighten it into some semblance of order.

"Come on, I'll take you back to the dorm," he said gruffly, not masking his annoyance very subtly.

The short drive to the campus passed in complete silence. Cale pulled the Bronco into the parking lot at the dormitory and prepared to get out.

"Don't bother walking me to my room," Allison broke in, before he opened his door. "I can find my own way."

A look of cold fury passed over Cale's face. He opened the door on his side and got out without saying a word to her. On the brief walk into the dorm and up the stairs, Cale moved beside her like some dark, angry giant, the coolness of his manner like the bite of the winter wind to her.

Allison went through the ritual of searching through her handbag for the key when she got to her door. She inserted it into the lock and turned the knob.

She finally looked up at Cale and tried to force a certain nonchalance into her tone. "I'm sorry about tonight, Cale, but I am glad we met again," she said, extending her hand in a gesture of friendship. "Good luck with your new book and take care." Allison was finding this more difficult than she had expected, especially when Cale stood there looking down at her without a word or the slightest expression on his face. "Well . . . good night, Cale," she murmured noncommittally.

He stood there a moment longer, then turned away, leaving a chill behind him.

"Good-bye, Allison," floated back to her as he disappeared around the corner of the stairway.

CHAPTER FIVE

The next two weeks were both the busiest and the loneliest of Allison's life. She filled her days with classes and her evenings with writing, but the nights were haunted by the image of one man—a man she had not seen since that fateful moment when he had turned his back and walked away from her.

If Allison had told herself once, she had told herself a hundred times that she was better off without Cale and the brief affair that would have surely followed as night follows day. But in the dead of night, alone in her bed, remembering the heat of his passion, the touch of his hands on her flesh, the look in his eyes as he gazed down into hers, it was sometimes impossible to convince herself she was indeed better off without him.

She could not fight the growing realization that Cale's brief appearance in her life was somehow a turning point for her. She felt a certain sense of poignancy when she recalled the way he had confided to her the story behind *Journey*. That they came from totally different backgrounds was true. That she had once been the teacher and he the student was true. But they had met now as a man and a woman, different and yet equal, and that was the truest of all.

Allison had her share of regrets. Her head told her this was the only reasonable way, but her heart knew that no man had stirred her body and mind as Cale had. She wondered if any man would again.

She had heard through the grapevine the day before that the renowned Christian Trent had apparently wrapped up his research at Dartmouth and had left the campus. The thought was far more devastating than she had imagined it would be. With it came the realization that the hope of seeing him again had been in the back of her mind all along. She had refused to admit it, until it was painfully clear that she would not see him again.

Allison nursed her grief in private, presenting a brave face to a world that had no idea what had occurred to her. If anyone suspected, it was Helen with her shrewd eyes and sixth sense. She had been sorry to say good-bye to Helen earlier that day and had promised to keep in touch.

Classes were over, evaluations completed, and with a full portfolio tucked under her arm, Allison returned to finish her packing. She was regretting her initial decision to drive to New Hampshire instead of flying in. Almost everyone had said good-bye and was already on the way home. She was one of a handful who were staying another night before leaving in the morning.

With a weariness born of sleepless nights and a general lack of enthusiasm for the long drive ahead of her, Allison dumped her handbag and portfolio on the bed and slumped down into a chair. She couldn't face eating dinner in a nearly deserted dining hall tonight; that would only serve to remind her how lonely she really was. She promised herself instead that as soon as she had her packing finished, she would treat herself to a package of cheese crackers and a cola from the vending machine in the dormitory lounge.

Clothes didn't pack themselves, she briskly reminded herself and got to her feet and went to work. Despite all that had happened in the past few weeks, Allison had no regrets. She didn't regret the decision to come to this writers' workshop and she did not regret meeting Cale again. It would be a memory she would tuck away and take out in the privacy of her own thoughts. If anything had come from this experience, it was a sharpening of her senses and a renewed sense of what was important in her life. She wanted to write, and she was more determined than ever to give herself that chance. In the end, she was the only one who could.

She had once told Cale that his success could be an inspiration to other writers. Well, his whole life and what he had accomplished despite the odds was an inspiration to Allison. If he could do it, then by God, in her own way she could too. At least, she was going to try, and that was a commitment she had never made before.

It took almost an hour for Allison to finish packing her suitcases. Then, as she had promised herself, she strolled down to the first-floor lounge and inserted the required coins into a vending machine for what was to be her dinner. The rest of the evening was spent laying out the things she would need the next day and putting her room to rights.

At ten o'clock, feeling tired and a little disheartened, she slipped off her clothes, put on a long, silky nightgown and climbed into the narrow single bed. She did not fall asleep immediately as she usually did, but lay there going through her schedule for the following morning step by step. It was one way to keep her thoughts from straying to the man she seemed to think of so often these days.

When the knock first came at the door of her dormitory room, Allison thought she was merely dreaming. Then it was repeated, louder and more insistent the second and third time. She glanced at the clock by her bed as she got up and saw that it was nearly midnight.

"Who is it?" she asked in a sleep-rusty voice, pressing her cheek to the wooden frame.

"Allison, it's Cale." The simple statement in that familiar deep, husky voice sent a quiver right down to her toes.

Allison turned the lock, opened the door a fraction of an inch, and peered through the crack she had created. It was unmistakably Cale Harding, looming in the hallway outside her room like some large, dark shadow. She opened the door wider, unmindful of her relative state of undress, and stared up at him without a word. While the puzzlement on her face no doubt came through clearly, he could not see the quickening beat of her heart.

"Cale, what are you doing here?" she asked, stifling a yawn behind her hand.

"I came back . . . oh, hell, I came back for this," he swore in a muffled groan as he swept her into his arms and brought his mouth down on hers with a ferocity that had her immediately awake and alert.

The suddenness of his action caught Allison unprepared. She found herself instinctively reacting to his kiss by hungrily kissing him back. She could not deny to herself or to Cale that she was as happy to see him as he apparently was to see her. Oh, God, it felt so good to be in his arms again. He held her against his chest, plundering her mouth for every bit of sweetness he could extract in a single breath.

Cale slowly released her mouth and the arms he grasped in his powerful hands. He tucked her into his shoulder, content to simply hold her there for a moment, to feel her safely within his embrace.

"Cale." His name came out in a small voice, muffled as it was by his shirt. "Cale, what are you doing here?" Allison reiterated as she put her head back and looked up at him.

Some dark emotion played across his features, which failed to yield the answer to her question. He let her go and stepped inside the room, closing the door behind him. A moment later, the room was flooded with light.

"Listen," he began, looking superciliously around, "do you mind if we sit down and talk for a while?"

There was a long silence. "Yes . . . I mean, no. Sit down, Cale," she amended. Suddenly realizing that her gown was rather revealing in this light, Allison picked up the matching negligee from the desk chair and slipped it on, indicating he could take that seat if he wished.

Cale unfurled his long legs and settled on the undersized piece of furniture, looking for all the world as if the room were too small to contain him. He studied his palms for a minute or two and then glanced up as Allison curled up on the bed, tucking her feet beneath her. She had little choice. Cale had the only available chair in the room.

He stared at her a moment longer, then swore again. He took a deep breath. "I had to see you, Allison. Hell, I was halfway up to the White Mountains when I did a U turn and came back."

The words came from Allison almost unconsciously. "I'm glad you did." It was the understatement of the year, but it was all she was willing to admit until Cale clarified his intentions. She was unsure of this man and even more of the part she played in his life—if any.

"I . . . ah came back—" Cale stopped cold and looked away. When his gaze swung back to her, Allison could tell he was a little uncomfortable. She realized it was one thing to write about life and another to actually live it. "The past two weeks have been pretty rough for me," he finally admitted in a guttural tone.

"I know what you mean," she replied, a touch of irony in her voice. She realized that she would have to give some indication of her feelings if she wanted him to continue. Allison took a deep, steadying breath. "I've missed you, Cale."

He looked her straight in the face. "And I have missed you. I finally figured out what was the matter with me, you see. I couldn't just go off like that knowing I wouldn't see you again." The words were delivered in a low voice, but she clearly heard every one.

"I wanted to see you again too, but after that night—" She hesitated to put it into words.

Cale ran his hands through the hair at the sides of his face in an agitated motion. "I wish you could understand, Allison, that I want you, not some memory, not some dream you imagine I've been chasing all these years. Yes, maybe I did have a thing about you then, but it isn't the same feeling I have now. You are an intelligent and beautiful woman. I can't help but desire you for those reasons, but it's more than that." Cale paused for a moment and seemed to be searching for the right words. "I'm not sure

I can explain. I'm not sure anyone can explain why two people are attracted to each other. Maybe it's chemistry, plain and simple. I just know it's there between us, and I don't want to walk away from it without giving it another chance. I won't wrap it up neat and pretty and try to pin a label on it, Allison, but I do think we should give it that chance." Cale stopped and waited for her to speak.

Allison closed her eyes and shuddered. She hadn't expected him to be so straightforward with her. It was rather frightening to her that he should be so. She was used to men who couched everything in pretty, if insincere, terms and his direct approach left her feeling adrift on an uncertain sea. She opened her eyes at last and discovered Cale was watching her every move, her slightest expression. He knew she was afraid. Allison could see it in the watchful eyes and in the hands that were unnaturally still on his lap.

"I don't know, Cale." She spoke in a voice barely above a whisper. "I thought you were on your way north to work on a book. I leave for New York in the morning. It seems rather senseless to talk about giving us a second chance when we're going to be hundreds of miles apart."

"But we don't have to be, honey." The endearment seemed to slip effortlessly from his lips. "I'm on my way to a writers' colony in the White Mountains. It's quiet and private and probably the best place to work that I've ever seen. If you are really serious about giving yourself the summer to write, what better place to do it? You could come with me, Allison." Cale could be very persuasive when he put his mind to it. "I know for a fact that there are several empty cabins and you'd be welcome to use one. And I promise that nothing will happen between the two of us unless you want it as much as I do. I want you to be with me, Allison," he said with a depth of feeling that caught her by surprise.

"It sounds wonderful, Cale. Really it does. But how can you be so sure that I'll be welcome? I'm not a well-known writer, or even in the same league as the people who must stay at a place like that."

"You'll be welcome, don't worry about that," he stated in a tone that would brook no argument. "This isn't quite like the MacDowell Colony at Peterborough, although it is just as secluded in its way."

"I don't even know what the MacDowell Colony is." Allison grimaced.

Cale leaned forward in his chair, his face becoming animated as he explained. "The MacDowell Colony was founded by the widow of Edward MacDowell, the composer, as a refuge for writers and artists and musicians. It's a secluded farm with a number of individual cabins similar to the place I've been working out of. The Colony was a haven at one time for people like Willa Cather, Thornton Wilder, Stephen Vincent Benét, and Edward Arlington Robinson, just to name a few. The colony up by the White Mountains is founded on the same principle—that an artist occasionally needs a quiet place to work away from the demands and interruptions of everyday life. You'd love it, Allison. I know you would," Cale stated with a conviction she found impossible to argue with.

"Perhaps I would," she replied absently, "but I'm due back in New York, Cale."

"Is there someone waiting for you?" he asked, suddenly realizing it was a possibility he had failed to consider up until now.

Allison sensed the tension in his body as he waited for

her to answer. "There is no one special waiting for me to return," she murmured, watching as the tenseness seemed to flow out of his large, steely frame. "I did tell my family and friends, however, to expect me back this week."

"You could always phone them and explain." Cale simplified the whole matter for her in a single sentence. "It would give you the opportunity you've always wanted as a writer, Allison. And it would give us a chance as well."

She sat there safely cocooned in her robe, wondering if she dared to take this step. She had been foolhardy and impulsive in her youth and it had never brought her anything but misery. But surely at thirty-two she was not so entrenched in living life safely that she no longer dared to take any chances, Allison argued with herself. She wanted to be with Cale and she wanted to write, and the opportunity to do both was being handed to her on a silver platter. The time had finally come when she had to make that decision and commitment. It was being thrust upon her now. She must decide—she alone.

Allison looked up at the man sitting on the edge of the desk chair and suddenly knew what her answer would be. She was too young to play it safe. There were never any guarantees in this life, she reminded herself unnecessarily.

"All right, Cale. I'll give it a try, anyway," she said, her voice holding an unsteady note.

"You won't regret your decision, honey. I promise you that," he said, looking almost triumphant as he smiled across the room at her. "We'll leave first thing in the morning."

"What will I do with my car? I know I don't have the right kind of clothes to go running off to the mountains."

She immediately thought of several stumbling blocks to their departure.

"I'll see to it before we leave that your car is taken care of." Cale sighed. "We can always stop and do whatever shopping you require at the local army-navy store before we set out. Now, is there anything else?" he asked, as if those were only minor irritations to be dealt with.

"I guess not," she replied, bestowing a hesitant smile on him. "I just hope I'm making the right decision."

"You are," he said, as if he had looked into some crystal ball and knew that it was so. He had enough self-assurance for both of them, it seemed.

"Do you have a place to stay tonight?" Allison inquired, coming back to practical matters.

"No, I don't," Cale replied, apparently not having thought of it until she asked.

"I suppose you could always stay here, but . . ." Allison trailed off as she glanced down at the single bed beneath her. She tried her best to envision the two of them sharing it, but the thought brought an amused smile to her lips. "Somehow I don't think the logistics are quite right," she finished on a droll note.

"We could always try what the guys in the dorm did when I was in college," Cale suggested, baiting her with aplomb.

"And what was that, Mr. Harding?" she said, taking the bait.

"If you will allow me to show you," he said, getting to his feet and coming to stand beside the bed.

Allison scooted off the edge of the mattress and watched with amazement as Cale proceeded to tear the bed apart. He first threw the mattress to the floor in the middle of the room and then lifted the box spring off its frame and put it down beside the mattress. What resulted, in a crude way, was a makeshift bed of double the original proportions.

"There! It may not be the most comfortable night either of us has spent, but I'm game if you are," Cale challenged, turning to catch her reaction to his redecorating efforts.

"I suppose it won't kill either of us for one night," Allison replied, her heart picking up speed as she realized the arrangement would put them in very close proximity for the night. "However, I take dibs on the mattress," she quickly put in. "You can have the springs. You must admit it beats sleeping on the bare floor," she added, pursing her lips with satisfaction.

"I'd sleep anywhere with you, sweetheart, and nary a word of complaint would cross these lips," Cale returned, tit for tat.

"Cale Harding . . ." That familiar tone of warning came into her voice.

"All right." He threw up his hands in mock surrender. "I promise to behave myself. But I'm not going to like it," he tacked on under his breath. "There are a few things I need from the truck. I'll be back in a few minutes," he announced, turning toward the door. "You might put the top sheet on the spring for me and find an extra blanket while I'm gone."

"I might." Allison folded her arms across her breasts as she watched him go out the door.

Despite the fact that she hated to be told what to do by anyone, Allison recovered her sense of humor while Cale was gone and spread the sheet over the box spring for him. She found a spare blanket in the closet and put it down on his side. When she stood back to admire her handiwork she realized with a renewed sense of apprehension the precarious position she had put herself in. She would be spending the next few hours practically in the same bed with Cale.

It wasn't that she was afraid of what Cale might do, but rather she was afraid of herself. The situation created a sense of intimacy that would not be lost on either of them. If he should decide to precipitate matters through persuasion, she wasn't at all sure she could say no to him. Common sense might dictate that was the only wise course to follow, but her common sense seemed to go right out the window where Cale Harding was concerned.

Well, dammit, then she would just have to keep a firm grip on herself and not do anything foolish, Allison told herself severely. She was a mature, strong-minded woman, not some easily persuaded youngster. She would stay on her side tonight and Cale on his. That's all there was to it!

She quickly made up the mattress for herself and was settled in for the night when Cale finally came back through the door, a duffel bag tossed over one shoulder. Allison watched through half-open eyes as he dropped the duffel bag in an out-of-the-way corner and began to unbutton his shirt, not once looking down to see if she were watching him. She squeezed her eyes shut more tightly when she realized he was unzipping his jeans. She heard his bare feet on the tile floor and then the click of the light switch. A moment later, she felt the springs beside her give way beneath his weight.

"Thanks for the sheet and blanket," Cale murmured,

his voice coming from nearby. "I guess we could both use whatever sleep we can get tonight."

"Yes. Good night, Cale," Allison said, her voice coming out soft and a little breathless much to her dismay.

She felt a movement beside her and then opened her eyes to see a dark form hovering above her.

"Good night, Allison," he repeated, his voice quiet, his breath warm against her skin.

Then Cale brought his mouth down to hers in a gentle and tender kiss, a kiss that asked for no display of passion and gave none. His fingers lightly caressed her cheek and her neck to one bare shoulder, but she could tell by his touch that Cale truly meant his good-night. He drew back from her and settled down on his half of the makeshift bed without another word.

The next thing Allison knew, Cale's breathing became regular and rhythmic. It seemed at least one of them wasn't going to have any difficulty getting to sleep! Allison abruptly turned onto her side, telling herself the emotion she was feeling was definitely *not* disappointment.

She awoke at what seemed to be nearly dawn. Gray light filtered into the room through the drapes. Apparently some time during the short night, she had sought the warmth and comfort Cale represented; Allison found herself snuggled up to his back, her arms wrapped around his waist, her face buried in the curve of his shoulder.

The problem, of course, was to disentangle herself from him without disturbing him. She wanted to remove all evidence of her nocturnal wanderings without Cale's knowledge. Allison tried to inch back onto the mattress, slowly withdrawing the arm about his waist. She scarcely dared to breathe during the painfully slow process.

She had very nearly succeeded when Cale rolled over in his sleep, one arm falling heavily across her breast, holding her prisoner as she lay in the crack between the box spring and the mattress.

Then just as Allison still had some small hope of getting herself out of the present predicament, Cale's eyes fluttered open and stared straight into her own.

"God, you're beautiful in the morning," he murmured, drawing her back into the full circle of his embrace.

"It's not morning," she pointed out, with a quick gesture at the gray light coming in the windows. She quit trying to move away when it suddenly dawned on her that Cale's arms was where she had wanted to be all along. Her subconscious had known that last night, even if she had not.

"You're right, it's not morning and it's not night," Cale said in a low voice that sent strange quivers down her spine. "It's that time between the two, the time when night creatures have crept away to their beds and day creatures have not yet awakened."

The timbre and rhythm of Cale's resonant baritone captured Allison's imagination as much as the actual words he was saying. She found herself mesmerized by the tone of his voice and by the look in the golden-brown eyes that held hers captive.

"Cale." She moved a little closer and pressed a kiss to the corner of his mouth, her body curving enticingly into his. The message she was sending him was loud and clear, unmistakable in its intent. She wanted him to kiss her.

Cale stiffened with wariness and grew unnaturally silent. Allison could feel the tautness of his body next to hers and knew he was trying to fathom the apparent change in her attitude.

"I don't think this is a good idea, Allison," Cale said in a tone that carried a warning in its resonant depths.

"Why not?" she almost whispered as she moved closer, bringing her mouth to within a fraction of an inch of his. She sensed he was waging some kind of battle with himself —knowing he should push her away from him and not wanting to in the same instant.

He turned the full force of his studied gaze on her upturned face. "I think you know why not," he said with a touch of reproach.

Allison inhaled a slow, trembling breath. "But I want you to kiss me," she boldly announced.

Cale made a slight inarticulate noise. "Are you sure, Allison?"

She did not need to ask the meaning behind his question. They both realized its significance. "Yes. I've never been more sure in my life," she murmured, her voice shaking with emotion.

They came together then with the full knowledge and understanding that neither was walking into this with eyes closed. Cale's mouth was warm and sleep-drugged on hers as he took what was so generously offered. Allison knew it was what he had wanted all along, and now she wanted it, too. His lips were soft and persuasive. Yet there was a hesitancy in the way he kissed her, as though he wanted her to know there was still time to change her mind without out any damage being done. But Allison knew that time was long past for her.

Although she came to him of her own free will, Cale did not try to hurry her response. With a leisurely and studied

111

grace, he rained a shower of light kisses on her lips and eyes and the tip of her nose without once trying to entice her into revealing the passion he surely knew was just beneath the surface.

Allison returned his kisses with butterfly-light caresses to each feature of the face she wanted to know better than any other. She traced an imaginary path across his cheekbone, around the full lips, and down the proud, jutting chin. It was a strong face—vitally alive and perfectly fashioned—as if a sculptor had deliberately set out to re-create the image of man at his best.

They both seemed aware of that heightened sense of expectancy, of wonder, that exists when two people first set out to discover all there is to know about each other. No kiss, no caress would be taken for granted in this exquisite search. Then their lips met with an insistency that made them move more quickly and thoroughly in their mutual exploration.

Cale seemed to find even the inch that separated them intolerable. He pulled Allison across his chest and molded her to his long frame with hands that caressed and soothed. He seemed to find pleasure in the simple fact that she conformed to his hardness with her own complementing softness.

As his mouth came up to meet hers, Allison eagerly gave entrance to his probing tongue, feeling a delicious curl of sensual excitement along every nerve ending of her body. Instinctively, she began to move against him, her mouth fulfilling his every request while making equal demands of its own. She ran her tongue, pink and moist, across his lips and down his neck to the shoulder beneath her, savoring the distinctive taste of his skin, wanting to take in the very essence of him.

Cale finally rolled her back onto the mattress and followed her, pinning her there beneath his tremendous weight. It was a weight Allison would gladly have borne a thousand times over. She found the sheer physical magnitude of the man an enticement. Even the strength in his hands excited her, hands she drew to her mouth as she proceeded to nibble the tip of each finger in turn. She pressed her lips into the palm of his hand and flicked her tongue back and forth until she felt him shudder at her touch.

She ran her fingertips along the wall of sinewy muscle that comprised his chest and abdomen and strayed for a moment to explore the firm flesh of each arm. He was smooth and powerful and tough as steel beneath her touch. That was enticement in itself. Where Cale was firm, it seemed she was soft, and Allison eagerly studied the contrast between them.

Then Cale became the rover, pushing aside the skimpy straps of her nightgown with one swift, sure motion. He trailed his lips along her bare flesh with a concentration that nearly drove her mad. He nipped at the skin between neck and shoulder and then inched lower to the rounded swell of her breasts.

With an intensity that shook Allison to the core of her being, he sought out the rosy buds that lay suppressed in the center of her breasts. At his first caress, they swelled into his hands, their hard peaks teasing his palms. He drew her alongside him and thrust out his tongue until it barely touched her nipple, lightly teasing it back and forth

113

until it grew and hardened even more under his erotic caress.

A small moan of intense pleasure escaped Allison's lips, telling him that she was nearing the point where pleasure became inexorably mixed with pain. Yet he still persisted, touching only the tip of her breasts, one after the other, with a feather-light touch that drove her to want him to do so much more.

"Cale—" She groaned his name aloud, trying to arch her body deeper into his, trying to force him to release her from his exquisite teasing.

"What is it, babe?" he said huskily, capturing her flesh between his teeth and giving it a gentle tug.

She threw her head back, the clean line of her arched throat only that much more inviting. "Cale, please! I can't take much more of this." She moaned, unconsciously moistening her parched lips.

He nearly drove her to the breaking point before he complied with her unspoken wish by suckling fully at each breast with a demand that released her from the edge of pain. His hands moved down her body, caressing her through the thin barrier of her gown. He drew it up around her waist, running his hand along the smooth length of her leg, caressing the sensitive inner line of her thigh.

Then all teasing disappeared as Cale seemed to realize he was losing control over his own desires. Allison felt the change in him as he rolled back on top of her and captured her face between his hands. He stared down into her eyes for a moment and then brought his mouth to hers in a kiss that seemed to last a lifetime. She felt the tension coiled up inside him and knew that he, too, must soon seek relief from this pleasure that was pain.

She ran her hands down his thighs and found herself wishing that the final barriers between them would magically disappear. She tugged impatiently at the waist of his shorts as he maneuvered the nightgown over her head. Cale finished the job by kicking off the last of his own garments, and they met for the first time bare flesh to bare flesh.

"I want you now, Allison," Cale muttered against her mouth, his tongue making one more wild foray into her. His body followed in imitation, finding her eager for him in all ways.

He pressed deeper into her with his tongue and with the strength of his manhood until he seemed to fill every part of her. He urged her on and on, asking for no quarter and giving none, taking her to the height of sexual excitement again and again and always pulling back just at the last possible moment.

Allison curled herself around him, holding him fast to her as he moved with thrusts that left them both without a breath in their bodies. She knew somehow she would not be able to stay with him, and she cried out in anguish when he let her go on without him. But then it began again, this time building to an even greater height, and they went the last step together, their bodies one as they reached for the stars and found the true meaning of oblivion.

Cale fell upon her, drained and mindless, feeling as though he had never really made love before and knowing the same was true for her. Allison curled up in his arms, content beyond anything she had ever imagined. This then was complete peace and contentment, this feeling of being in total harmony with another human being, this sharing the most intimate secrets of herself and finding it reciprocated in kind.

Making love was an act of trust. It revealed the greatest vulnerability between a man and a woman who sought to find a moment of eternity with each other. It was an exchange of the greatest gift there was.

Allison gazed up into the face posed above her, feeling the tears break loose from her eyes to slip down her cheeks. "Oh, Cale . . . I . . . I . . ." She swallowed with difficulty, unable to go on, unable to find the words she wanted so desperately to say.

"Shhhh, babe," he murmured, consoling her with his gentleness. "I know, I know. It's never been like that for me either. Maybe there are some things that can't be put into words," he said thoughtfully. "Maybe we shouldn't even try." Then Cale rolled onto his side and held her closely to him. "Sleep awhile, my love, just sleep."

But Allison had already drifted into the sleep of complete fulfillment and did not hear his soothing entreaty.

CHAPTER SIX

When Allison awoke again, she knew instantly it must be mid-morning from the bright sunlight pouring in through the windows. Disoriented, she lay there for a minute or two without stirring, unsure of where she was or why she was on the floor.

Then the events that had taken place earlier that morning rushed to the fore of her consciousness, and she quickly turned to see if Cale was still beside her. She experienced a moment of supreme disappointment when she discovered he was not. It would have been lovely to awaken in his arms, but perhaps this was the best way after all, she rationalized. It gave them both a little breathing space after the intimacy they had shared only hours before.

It did not enter her mind at first that Cale might be gone permanently. When the possibility hit Allison, it hit hard. She jumped up, wrapping the sheet around her nude form, and took a quick survey of the room. The box spring was back on the bed frame, the sheet and blanket Cale had used last night were neatly folded and stacked on the desk chair, the duffel bag he had tossed in the corner was no longer there. It was as if every shred of evidence proving he had ever been there had been carefully removed.

She could not bring herself to believe that Cale could make love to her as he had just hours before and then simply skip town. The whole notion was perfectly absurd! Yet it occurred to her that all the evidence was pointing in that direction.

Then out of the corner of her eye, Allison caught a glimpse of a piece of paper propped up against the makeup mirror on the dresser. For a moment, her heart seemed to cease beating. She dashed across the room and grabbed the paper. It was a note from Cale, written in a bold, sprawling, masculine hand, telling her he had gone to see about storing her car and would be back by ten o'clock.

Allison did not realize until she began to breathe again that she had been holding her breath all the while she was reading. She gave a nervous little laugh and called herself several ridiculous names out loud. He was doing exactly what he had promised to do—he was seeing to the matter of her car before they left for the mountains. But a small inner voice reminded her that she had been truly afraid for just a moment that she had lost him.

She read through the note a second and third time, fingering the signature where he had written, "Love, Cale." It struck her then that she might well be getting involved in far more than an affair with this man. Earlier that morning, she had thought only of the fact that she wanted Cale Harding as she had wanted no other man. The possibility of falling in love had not occurred to her.

But Allison considered that possibility now. Was it conceivable that she might actually be falling in love with Cale? Love took nurturing, love took time, and that was

118

one thing she and Cale had never had. She had learned from past experience not to trust her own instincts when it came to love. She had been deadly wrong on more than one occasion, and she could be wrong this time as well.

She was standing in the middle of the dorm room, wrapped in a bedsheet, wondering what in the world she was going to do about the situation, when she glanced up at the clock on the bedside table and saw it was nearly ten. Unless she wanted Cale to return and find her as she was now, dressed in only a sheet, she had better get a move on it.

Allison took only enough time for a quick shower and then slipped into a pair of designer pants and matching top in a shade of pale lavender. She hurried through her morning ritual of doing her makeup and hair, keeping in mind that Cale could walk through the door at any moment.

With five minutes to go, she decided the next task at hand was putting the room into some semblance of order. She folded the sheet and blanket she had used and added them to the pile started by Cale. Then she picked up one end of the mattress and struggled to get it back into position on the bed. With that done, the dormitory room took on its normal appearance. Allison had to admit she was feeling a little self-conscious about facing him, but at least she could do so now without tripping over her own mattress.

She was packing the last of her things in an overnight bag when a soft knock sounded at the door. She straightened up from her task and crossed the room to answer the summons she had known was coming. She turned the knob and pulled the door open.

How many times in their brief relationship had she gone

to this very door and found Cale standing on the other side? Yet each time she did so, Allison felt her heart lurch at the sight of him. There was something about Cale that quickened her pulse rate and left her a little breathless.

He stood gazing down at her from his great, towering height, dressed in casual jeans and a cotton shirt. A broad smile broke across the handsome features as he took a step toward her, gathering her into his arms in a gesture that said far better than any words that he was glad to see her.

Allison was not one to let her guard down frequently, but she found herself responding to him as if it were the most natural thing in the world. She slipped her arms around his waist and hugged him back, realizing anew the joy in the touch of another human being who cared. Cale seemed to have the ability to make her feel that little else mattered besides the two of them—not what other people thought or even what the world thought, but only that the world could sometimes exist between two people.

"Good morning, again," he murmured, gazing down into her face with an expression of tenderness.

Allison wished she could tell him how much that meant to her. He had thrilled her beyond anything she had ever imagined. Yet she knew they could be friends as well as lovers, and that was a gift beyond compare. She suddenly realized that Cale was one of the few men in her life who took her seriously. He had not scoffed at the idea that she wanted to do something with her life besides spend it as an ornament of some ambitious man. She had her own ambitions, and she sensed that he not only recognized that fact, but encouraged it. He was a special man in so many ways.

Cale touched his mouth to hers in a kiss that was gentle

and tender and perfect in its way. It reassured her that he had not taken the intimacy between them for granted.

"Good morning, yourself," Allison said, smiling up at him as he released her. "I'm just about ready, as you can see." She made a sweeping gesture of the room. "Were you able to find a place to store my car?"

"Yes, there's a garage not far from here that has room to keep it. We can drop it off on our way out of town. I take it that flashy Porsche sitting in the parking lot with the New York license is yours."

"Yes, that's mine," Allison confessed, grinning at him. "It's all part of the image, you know. Do you like it?"

"Well, I don't know about the image, but I rather like the woman behind it," he said in a tone that dripped with innuendo. Then Cale seemed to note for the first time the designer clothes she was wearing. A small crease appeared between his darkly accented brows. "Is that the kind of stuff you plan to wear in the mountains?" he asked with an air of incredulity.

"Yes. Outfits like this and several pairs of jeans, of course," Allison replied, looking down at the beautifully made garments, which were typical of her wardrobe. "Why? What's wrong with what I'm wearing?" She sniffed defensively.

Cale brushed his hand across his eyes. "Well, I think the first stop we need to make after we drop off your car is the local army-navy store. I don't suppose you brought any hiking boots with you or warm sweaters or a rain poncho . . ."

Allison looked at him as if he were half crazed. "I don't own a pair of hiking boots, and I would scarcely think to pack warm sweaters in the middle of the summer. As for the rain poncho—" She shuddered at the mere thought, unable to go on. It was becoming abundantly clear to her that Cale's idea of necessities was entirely different from her own. The staple of her wardrobe was a series of chic little black dresses for evening and a closetful of tailored designer suits for daytime. She couldn't imagine what one did with a rain poncho.

"Well, don't let it worry you, honey," he said with a crooked smile. "We can outfit you with everything you could possibly need in the mountains for about the same price as that get-up you're wearing, if my guess is right."

"Get-up! Do you have any idea what this get-up cost me?" Allison heard herself hoot. "This get-up, as you seem so fond of calling it, carried a price tag of five hundred dollars, Mr. Harding."

"Then all the more reason, my dear Miss Saunders, to pack it away until you return to civilization," he retorted in a low, mocking tone. "Now, if your bags are ready, I'll take them down to the Bronco while you see about checking out of this place."

"Everything has been taken care of," she informed him in a voice as stiff as her back. "All I have to do this morning is turn in the key to my room."

"Well, let's get going then, sweetheart. I am about to take you on the shopping spree of your life!"

They emerged from the local army-navy store an hour later loaded down with packages. Allison decided that a woman never really knew a man until she had gone shopping with him. In the space of one hour, Cale had picked out enough utilitarian jeans, shirts, sweaters, socks—even a rain poncho—to last her two lifetimes.

He explained that the laundry facilities at the colony

were a bit primitive and that she would find she needed every article of clothing he had insisted on buying. She was stunned by the amount of shopping he had managed to cram into a mere sixty minutes. It frequently took her longer than that to decide on one dress.

Cale loaded her packages into the back of the Bronco and politely helped her into the passenger seat. He remarked it was a good thing he had insisted she change into one of her new outfits right there in the store. Allison felt slightly strange dressed in a checked-cotton shirt, stiff new jeans, and a pair of socks. Good God, she hadn't worn a pair of socks since she was a little girl! The most expensive purchase of the morning, still only half the cost of her casual shoes, was a pair of leather hiking boots.

She did not feel or look at all like herself. Still, this was a new adventure for her, and Allison found herself experiencing a sense of excitement and expectancy that had been missing from her life for far too long. She was off to a place unlike any she had ever been with a man who was unlike any she had ever known. She was determined to be a good sport, come what may.

"If you don't mind, I think we should grab a bite of lunch at one of those drive-in places and eat on the way," Cale suggested as he pulled away from the store. "I heard on the radio this morning we could be in for some heavy rain this afternoon. I'd like to be at the colony before it hits."

"That's fine with me," Allison replied, reminding herself she was going to be a good sport and realizing she was famished besides. Any food sounded good to her at the moment.

With their hamburgers and French fries in hand, Cale began to drive north toward the White Mountains.

"This is beautiful country," Allison finally remarked, sitting back in her seat.

"Do you know much about this region of New Hampshire?" Cale asked, his tone only half humorous.

"No . . . but I have a funny feeling you're about to enlighten me." She chuckled, her mouth twisting into a wry smile.

"None of us is ever too old to learn, Miss Saunders," he said, lifting one eyebrow. Then he launched into his narrative with enthusiasm. "The White Mountains represent the highest elevations in the Northeast, for your information."

"And why are they called the White Mountains?" she asked, deciding to play along with him.

"Actually, it's very simple. They're named for the grayish-white taller peaks in the range. Of course, they don't compare in size with the Rockies, but there's a certain grandeur about them that is incomparable. Up by Gorham is Mt. Washington, the highest peak east of Colorado and north of the Smokies. It was first seen by the white man over 370 years ago and is still a source for myth and mystery. On the western slope of Mt. Washington is the site of the first mountain-climbing railroad in the world. It's been running since 1869 and is still used today. For the experienced hiker—" Cale looked down at her shiny new hiking boots and stiff jeans and smiled to himself as if something had tickled his funnybone. "As I was saying, for the experienced hiker there is the Appalachian Trail, which winds around nearly the entire White Mountains

with a chain of huts, hostels actually, which are about one day's hike apart. But that is definitely not for the novice."

"Are you inferring that I am a novice?" she said loftily.

"It's nothing the right teacher couldn't take care of, honey," Cale said with a perfectly straight face. "There are certain points of interest you shouldn't miss as long as you're here," he went on. "There's the Old Man of the Mountains in Franconia Notch State Park. That might be of particular interest to you if you've read Hawthorne's story 'Great Stone Face.' It was based on the natural rock formation there. And not far from the Profile, as it is also known, is the Flume, a natural chasm formed about 200 million years ago. You really shouldn't miss the local sights while you're up here, Allison."

"But I'm coming up here to write, and I know you have a book to work on. We won't have time to play tourist, will we?" Allison was beginning to wonder just how long Cale expected her to stay. It was already the second week of July, and she had every intention of being back in New York by the end of the summer. "You know, I have to be back in the city this summer, Cale."

"Yeah, I know," he muttered, taking a long draught of the coffee from the paper cup in his hand. "We can't work all the time though. Don't you find that new places and new people keep your imagination alive as a writer?" He appealed to her on the basis of her work.

"Well, when you put it like that, how can I refuse?" she said, turning to him with a grin that said she had not been in the least fooled by his tactics.

Allison settled back in her corner of the Bronco and gazed out at the breathtaking scenery as they began their ascent into the mountainous regions. Green grasslands dotted with small towns were on either side of the high-way. Beyond were the foothills and farther still the towering peaks of the White Mountains loomed in the distance. There was a grandeur, a certain air of mystery about this place that made it fertile ground for the writer's imagination.

"This must be quite a ski area in the winter," speculated Allison, recognizing that the tracks going up the sides of the mountains were chairlifts.

"This is one of the most popular resort areas in this part of the country during the snow months," Cale affirmed. "In fact, if it gets too crowded, I think I'll head for some other place to work for the winter."

"Do you have a home someplace?" Allison suddenly realized she didn't know even that much about Cale.

"I've been staying in a hotel suite when I'm in New York, but otherwise I don't have a place of my own. I've been toying with the idea of buying in Connecticut, if I can find something I like. I don't know—" Cale paused and stared down into his half-empty cup for a moment. "Sometimes I like the idea of putting down roots, and then other times I like the freedom I have to travel and work wherever it strikes my fancy."

"Isn't that an awfully lonely way to live?" she murmured, trying to imagine her life without her small, luxurious apartment and the circle of friends she had made over the years. She couldn't imagine living out of a suitcase or a Bronco, as the case seemed to be for Cale.

"Writing is inherently a lonely profession, Allison. You'll soon discover that for yourself if you stick with it. Where you live is of little consequence when you spend ten

hours a day at a typewriter." He seemed determined to dispel any myths she might harbor.

"I suppose you're right," she said, mollified by his statement. She hadn't thought of it in quite that light before, but she realized he was no doubt speaking the truth.

"I don't mean to put you off when you're just starting out," Cale added after a moment. "But you might as well face the fact that being a professional writer is often a singularly lonely occupation. For some of us, the rewards outweigh the disadvantages, and then there are always those who seem driven to write. I once heard a very popular Australian novelist remark that there were basically two kinds of people who write: those who couldn't talk to other people and those who had so much to say that it just naturally overflowed onto paper. Maybe she was right."

"And which kind are you?" Allison asked, interested and curious.

"I suppose I'm in the first group," Cale admitted after some thought. "It has never been particularly easy for me to talk with other people. Like most children, I always felt that I was different. But in my case, I never outgrew that feeling. A lot of the time I was growing up there simply wasn't anyone to talk to," he said with a shrug, not asking for sympathy. It was merely a statement of fact. Allison had noticed on other occasions that he had the unique ability to talk about his background without the bitterness she was sure she would have felt in his place.

"I don't think I fit into either group entirely," she said, pausing to think about it. "Sometimes I need to be with other people, and sometimes I need to be alone."

"Oh, damn!" Cale swore irritably.

Allison gave a violent start. "What is it?" she finally found the courage to ask.

"There," Cale muttered, pointing ahead of them.

It took her several moments before she realized to what he was referring. Then she, too, saw the black rain clouds hovering around the mountain peaks in the distance.

"I was hoping we could make it to the cabins before it started," he explained, his face taking on a judicial look. "Some of these roads are treacherous enough in good weather, and it has been known to snow up in the higher regions every month of the year."

"Snow? In July?" Allison repeated incredulously.

"It's not impossible, just improbable," Cale said noncommittally. "Chances are we'll get away with nothing more than a good drenching."

Allison made a distasteful grimace. She had never been the type to put up with inclement weather and had considered on more than one gray New York day moving to a more temperate clime. In fact, if she had not grown up and always lived in the New York area, she would probably have picked a place like Phoenix, where the sun nearly always shone.

By the time Cale had driven into the forested region where the White Colony was located, it had started to rain in earnest. Gray drizzle was coming down in sheets. But if anything surprised Allison it was the fact that she didn't feel the least bit nervous about the change in the weather. She decided it had something to do with the confidence Cale managed to instill in people. How could anything go wrong with a great grizzly bear of a man like Cale Harding at her side? It was a comforting thought.

"We'll be approaching the colony as soon as we drive

through the creek," Cale announced above the clamor of the rain, the swish of the windshield wipers, and the roar of the engine. They waded across a shallow creek bed that ran perpendicular to the road.

All around them were tall northern pines and ground scrub. The scent of wet leaves permeated the air. It was almost cozy in the Bronco with the two of them snug inside and the storm raging without. It wasn't until they reached a large clearing and faint lights became visible through the curtain of rain that Allison realized they would soon be out in that cold, drenching rain.

She could see the vague outline of a cabin here and there set some distance apart among the trees. In the center of the clearing was the main lodge and dining room.

"I think we better both go to my cabin for now," Cale suggested smoothly. "This isn't ideal weather to go traipsing around trying to get you settled in your own place. We can always see to that once the rain lets up."

"I couldn't agree with you more," Allison said with feeling, looking out at the sheet of slate-gray rain.

Cale drove across the compound and parked the Bronco alongside one of the far cabins. Allison could see it was an actual log cabin and not merely a cottage. She watched as Cale turned around in his seat and pulled a poncho out from behind him. He slipped it over his head, adjusting the hood for full protection.

"If you can locate that smallest brown package in the bundle we bought this afternoon, you'll find your poncho inside," he commented. "I'd say you're going to need it. I'll go on ahead and unlock the door and turn on the lights. Then I'll come back for you." He swung the duffel bag over his arm and got out of the Bronco.

"Yes sir," Allison mumbled under her breath as she turned to comply. She had no wish to get soaked to the skin simply out of defiance.

The lights went on in the cabin. It was only a matter of minutes before she observed a tall, dark form coming back through the rain toward her. Cale swung the passenger door open and peered inside.

"Are you ready to make a run for it?" he said with grim humor.

"Ready as I'll ever be," Allison grumbled, momentarily forgetting the promise she had made herself about being a good sport. She clasped the overnight bag in one hand, her handbag in the other, and awkwardly stepped down from the Bronco.

"Let's go!" Cale took her by the arm, slamming the door of the four-wheel-drive vehicle shut behind her, and off they went.

"Oh!" she moaned once they were safely inside the cabin. "I'm all wet!"

"You'll dry out, honey," Cale chuckled, shaking his own poncho before pulling it over his head and hanging it on a hook on the back of the door. "It's only water, Allison," he said with a touch of impatience. "Here, let me help you with that." He took the bags from her hands and set them out of the way. Then he reached out and in one fluid motion had her poncho removed with the least amount of damage.

Allison gave her head a shake, licking the rain from her lips, and glanced up at him. "Thank you. I'm afraid I haven't quite got the hang of that contraption yet," she said, referring to the one-piece rain garment.

"Look around if you like. I'll slip into the kitchen and make us a cup of coffee," he said, suddenly playing the host.

"A cup of coffee sounds wonderful," she called after him, for the first time taking a good look at the cabin.

Allison had guessed it would hardly be the St. Regis, but she wasn't prepared for the primitive surroundings in which she now found herself. The cabin was rustic, that was for sure. She supposed it had a certain charm if one liked that sort of thing—hardwood floors with an occasional throw rug, rough log walls, a stone fireplace that was obviously not decorative, and plain, over-stuffed furniture. Liveable enough, she supposed, but hardly her idea of home.

The only compensation was a large, ornate desk and an overhead lamp situated in one corner of the room. She wandered over to the desk, idly fingering the keys of the electric typewriter set on its scarred surface, and absently read through the titles of the reference books Cale had stacked to one side.

She peeked around the corner and found that the next room was Cale's bedroom. It was average size, but it contained one of the largest beds she had ever seen. She supposed a man of Cale's stature would find a regular double bed a little restricting. It was certainly big enough for two, she thought, and then blushed at the thought.

That left only the bathroom at the end of the hall and the kitchen. Her curiosity satisfied, Allison made her way to the kitchen at the back of the cabin.

As it turned out, it was the one room that held a pleasant surprise for her. It was neat and compact and decorated in a bright, cheerful yellow. She was doubly surprised by the modern conveniences it had, right down to a small dishwasher and a microwave oven.

Cale was standing with the refrigerator door open, studying its contents. He turned as he heard her enter the room. "I asked the housekeeper to stock up on a few things for me, and I see she didn't forget, bless her little absentminded heart. I thought you might be hungry."

"I'm not really hungry, but that coffee certainly smells delicious," she commented, giving a nod in the direction of the drip coffeemaker on the counter.

With a leisurely grace that said he was perfectly at home in the kitchen, Cale took two mugs from the cupboard and poured them each a cup. "Well, what do you think of the place?" he inquired with an expectant air as they took a seat at the small kitchen table.

"Will my cabin be similar to this one?" she asked, avoiding a direct answer.

"Yes, they're all pretty much the same. I had a special bed put in mine and some of them have two bedrooms, but otherwise there isn't much difference in the cabins."

"I imagine it's quite cozy in the winter with a blazing stack of logs in the fireplace," Allison ventured to guess, not really knowing what else to say.

"It's not what you were expecting, is it?" Cale gave her a quick, shrewd look.

Allison found his simple inquiry difficult to answer. "I assumed it would be rustic." She picked her words with care, knowing he was following every syllable with the closest attention. "You can't expect me to do back flips,

132

Cale. I'm a city girl. I always have been. This is . . . different, that's all. I'm sure once the rain stops and I get settled in my own cabin, I'll feel better about the place," she said, deciding that honesty was the best policy.

"I'm only asking for one thing, Allison," he said with a flicker of his eyes. "Give it a fair chance."

"I'll try," she said, her brows drawn into a thoughtful frown.

Cale's face relaxed into a smile. "I don't know about you, honey, but I'm hungry! We can either try to make it across to the lodge or have one of my superb omelets right here. What do you say?"

Allison gazed out the kitchen window at the rain still coming down in a steady, gray stream. She turned back to him and injected an enthusiasm into her voice she wasn't at all sure she felt. "I cast my vote for the omelets."

"Somehow I thought you might," he replied with a chuckle, getting to his feet. "If you would like to freshen up before we eat, the bathroom is just down the hall."

Allison ran her hands over the mop of damp hair and made a face. "I must look a fright." She swallowed, realizing the extent of the damage done by the wind and rain.

"You always look gorgeous to me, lady," Cale murmured, dropping a light kiss on her upturned face. "Now run along and do whatever it is that you do. This kitchen is only big enough for one cook."

For once she was more than happy to do as she was told. As she left the kitchen, she could hear Cale whistling softly under his breath as he took a carton of eggs from the refrigerator and went to work. She took her own good time repairing the damage done to her makeup and hair and arrived back in the kitchen just as Cale was turning out two perfect omelets onto their plates.

The table was set with a small vase of wildflowers in the center and two sparkling glasses of wine. Allison was touched by all the trouble Cale seemed to have gone to for her benefit.

"Where did you find fresh flowers in this rain?" she asked in a hushed tone, bending over to inhale their fragrance. They carried the scent of the forest with them. Then she noticed that Cale's hair was a shade darker, as if he had just come from the shower, and she suddenly knew where the flowers had come from. Allison placed a hand on his arm and reached up to touch his face with her lips. "Thank you," she murmured, her voice cracking in the middle.

Cale appeared almost embarrassed for a minute, then he announced in a brisk tone that their dinner was ready. The omelets were deliciously light and fluffy, the wine chilled and robust. In all, Allison found it to be one of the most delightful dinners of her life.

Their conversation was just as brisk, ranging from a discussion of wines they had known and loved to the books they had recently enjoyed. They went on to a friendly disagreement concerning the current political scene. The time passed so quickly that Allison was stunned when she looked out and realized it was night. A quick glance at her watch confirmed that more than several hours had slipped by without her knowledge. And it was still raining cats and dogs, she groaned inwardly.

"This is turning into a damned monsoon," Cale muttered, coming up to stand beside her. "You must be tired, honey. Let's go to bed. We can see about your luggage and cabin in the morning."

Something in his tone made Allison glance up at him, but his expression told her nothing. "All right, Cale," she finally said, knowing it was the only reasonable course of action to follow. "I guess I am tired after that short night last night . . ." Her voice trailed off as a hot, unstoppable blush spread right up to her ears.

"I didn't know a mature woman of thirty still blushed," he said, a teasing undertone to his voice.

"I'm thirty-two, and as far as I know blushing recognizes no age limit," she countered, sounding faintly dismayed.

"Come on," he cajoled. "I'll even let you have the bathroom first tonight." Cale slipped a casual arm around her shoulders and steered her away from the window.

When he sauntered into the bedroom a half hour later, Allison was already settled in the king-size bed, the covers up around her neck.

"I think it's finally stopped raining," Cale remarked, opening the window an inch or two before tossing off his robe and getting in beside her.

Allison waited rather nervously, but he made no move to come any closer. She began to relax when she realized he had no intention of taking advantage of their situation. Yet she was still lying there no closer to sleep a good twenty minutes later.

"What's the matter?" came the deep, resonant voice beside her.

"It's the noise." She sighed. Then she went on, a kind of desperation in her voice. "I can't seem to get to sleep."

135

"The noise? But there isn't any noise out here." He laughed softly.

"That's the problem," Allison said with a sort of groan. "There isn't anything but complete silence. It's keeping me awake. I'm used to being lulled to sleep by the sounds of cars and buses and blaring horns. You know, the general bustle of the city."

"Well . . . I do a few birdcalls and a rather poor impersonation of Groucho Marx, or so I'm told," Cale said, pushing himself up on the pillow into a half-sitting position. "I suppose I could always try a traffic jam."

Allison's laughter bubbled to the surface like sparkling champagne. "Do you know you're really a very funny man?" She gulped, pulling herself together with a visible effort.

His expression darkened to a playful scowl. "Do you mean funny ha-ha or funny weird?" he asked, with more than a hint of suspicion in his voice.

"A little of both, I'd say." She coughed, trying to choke back her laughter.

Cale bent over her in the dark and ran his hand along her bare shoulder. Next his mouth found the sweet warmth of hers in a kiss that held the promise of an alternate solution to her insomnia.

"This is no laughing matter, Allison," he pronounced in an impatient tone when he realized the rapid rise and fall of her breasts was in no way due to any passion he was arousing.

"If you say so, Mr. Harding," Allison teased. Then her giggles died in mid-kiss, only to be replaced by greater emotion.

When Cale raised his head some minutes later, his voice

was low and rather husky. "What, you're not laughing, Miss Saunders?"

"No." Allison groaned, pulling his head back down to hers. "As you said, this is no laughing matter." Then she kissed him thoroughly and completely, with the knowledge that the best was yet to come.

CHAPTER SEVEN

The next morning dawned bright and clear with scarcely a sign of the previous day's downpour beyond an occasional mud puddle. Allison was soon situated in her own cabin, a near twin of the one Cale had only a short distance away. She spent that first day unpacking her belongings and getting settled in, having sent Cale away to work on his book, knowing he had to work even though she was there.

She set her portable typewriter on the desk in the front room of the cabin, stacking a ream of paper beside it, deciding it at least *looked* professional. There was a standard dictionary and a thesaurus on the small bookcase next to the desk, and she discovered a rather extensive library of reference books in the lodge strictly for the benefit of the in-residence writers.

Allison did not see Cale again that day until nearly evening. He strolled over to her cabin and asked if she would like to have dinner with him at the lodge. It was a rather odd arrangement, when in essence she was having a love affair with him, but she was quickly learning that the normal rules of the game did not apply here.

She agreed to have dinner with him, and as a consequence met several of the other renowned artists working at the colony that summer. Allison had to admit to a certain sense of awe when she realized she was actually talking with people whose names up until then had been merely signatures on best-selling books and hit Broadway plays. She spent a delightful evening listening to the flow of brilliant conversation, rarely finding the nerve to add anything of her own and often feeling very much the amateur. At least she no longer felt self-conscious in the jeans and shirts Cale had insisted she buy. They were almost a uniform at the colony.

By the end of the first week, Allison felt she was beginning to understand the special nature of this retreat. Socializing was only an occasional indulgence. People were here to work and that meant hours of isolation for most of them. If they weren't working and wanted to be with other residents, they went to the lodge. Otherwise, they left each other alone. It was the first rule of their unspoken code.

In the beginning, the discipline of spending nearly all day and even part of the evening writing was difficult for Allison. She was often restless, on occasion lonely, and frequently so tired by nightfall that she sometimes found herself hoping that Cale would not come by to see her. But nearly every night he sauntered over and invited her for a cup of coffee or a glass of wine, and then seemingly without fail one of them would end up spending the night in the other's cabin.

Sometimes they did no more than sleep in each other's arms, but more often they would end the evening or start the day by making love—at times with a wild desperation and other times with a gentleness and reverence for the force growing between them.

Despite the isolation and inconvenience of living in a remote area, Allison had never been happier in her life. She missed her friends and being able to go to a play or out to dinner at a four-star restaurant, but the sharp contrast between her normal life-style and living at the White Colony still held her in thrall. In the back of her mind was the knowledge that she could not live this way permanently, but it was refreshing for a change.

The only fear nagging at her heart was the realization that she was becoming far too attached to Cale. That would complicate matters when the time came for her to leave this place, and leave it she must in the end. And so she tried to savor those times they talked and walked or read or listened to music on the radio in a companionable silence.

Neither of them spoke of love or commitment, but Allison knew that the man was working his way into her heart and mind and soul as well as her body. Fear only reared its head when one had something to lose; she suddenly realized she did not want to lose Cale.

For the first time in a very long time, Allison began to think in terms of commitment—commitment to more than just a profession, but to a man and to a life-style very different from her own. She tried to tell herself that Cale had no intention of spending the rest of his life in these mountains, beautiful as they were. Perhaps, just perhaps, she could convince him to spend the greater part of his time in New York.

Then all the seemingly insurmountable problems that went along with that idea would start to give her a headache, and she would decide that the best policy for now was to take each day as it came and let tomorrow worry about itself. They lived totally in the present, taking no time to reflect on the past and half afraid to try to peer into the future.

Cale seemed more than content with their arrangement, and Allison sometimes thought to herself that he had no reason not to be. She had made it very easy for him—coming to the colony where he wanted to be, making no demands on his time or temperament that would distract him from his work. They were living in a fantasy. She grumbled occasionally that his writing took too much of him, but only to herself and only in the privacy of her own cabin, never to Cale.

She took solace in her own writing, discovering as so many others had before her that it was the best form of catharsis for the troubled heart. And so she finally began to write stories about real people and real emotions. Stories she would have been incapable of producing before she met Cale Harding again. Bemused, she realized their roles had switched—he was the teacher now and she the student.

The weather was beautiful all that week and most of the next until one morning it began to rain at dawn. It was one of those rains that would fall softly all day, saturating the earth with moisture and the air with the scent of pine.

Allison had been at the typewriter since eight o'clock that morning, working right through the lunch hour without a thought to food. Her fingers were literally flying across the keys, trying to capture her thoughts as quickly as they came to her. She finally took a short break, stretching her tired back muscles as she walked to the kitchen to make herself a cup of hot tea. She was sitting rereading what she had managed to write when a knock came at the cabin door.

It startled her for a minute. No one went calling around here at this time of day and certainly not without a specific invitation. Allison put her teacup down on the desk and went to answer the door.

"Coming!" she said loud enough to be heard over the soft patter of rain on the roof and through the thickness of the wooden door. She swung the door open and beheld a rather sheepish-looking Cale standing on her threshold.

"Hello," he said, unsure of his welcome, knowing his visit was an intrusion upon her privacy and went against the unwritten code of the colony. The fact that in some ways he never took her or their relationship for granted endeared him all the more to Allison.

"Hello." She smiled up at him.

"Am I interrupting anything?" he asked, and then answered his own question with a dark scowl that marred his features. "Of course, I am."

"No, really. I was taking a break, anyway. In fact, I was just having a cup of tea. Would you like to come in and join me?" she asked, taking a step back.

"No, thanks, I don't think so. Actually, I thought I might take a walk. I was beginning to get cabin fever," he replied, referring to one of the hazards of the trade. "Would you like to come with me?"

Allison looked out and nearly said "In this rain?" But she thought better of it. Cale had sought her out because he needed her. She was aware of that from the tired expression around his eyes and the way they seemed to silently ask for her understanding. Besides, if she did get wet she would dry out.

"Let me get my boots and poncho," she finally responded, turning back into the room.

Cale carefully stepped inside, making sure he stayed on the rug by the front door. Allison slipped off the pair of sandals she was wearing and replaced them with her socks and hiking boots. Without once stopping to catch a glimpse of herself in the mirror, she pulled the poncho over her head and announced she was ready.

Where had her vanity disappeared to? she thought as they walked out the cabin door and into the rain. Here she was dressed in wrinkled jeans and an ugly army-green poncho, her hair braided down the back of her head, scarcely a speck of makeup on her face, and she wasn't the least bit concerned. She was becoming a slob and it didn't even bother her, and *that* did bother Allison. She seemed to be losing some part of herself up here in the mountains. She could only hope the gains outweighed the losses.

They strolled for some time without speaking, heading down a trail that wound back through the wooded area surrounding the clearing. Allison put her face up to catch a drop of rain on her tongue, dislodging her hood in the process. It fell back from her head. She did not bother replacing it, allowing the cool, soothing rain to wash her face and hair.

"Hey, what do you think you're doing?" Cale laughed, the first laugh she had heard from him that afternoon. "You're getting all wet."

"I won't melt, and besides, I've always done what a mature, responsible woman my age was supposed to do and I'm tired of it," she declared with a vehemence rare

143

for her. "If I want to get all wet, then, by God, I'll damned well get wet!"

"Yes, ma'am!" Cale replied with what sounded suspiciously like a chuckle. "Far be it for me to tell you how to live your life. You go right ahead and make your declaration of independence."

"Maybe it is a declaration of independence," Allison responded, impishly sticking her tongue out at him. "And maybe it's about time—even long overdue. As children we're always learning how to grow up to become responsible adults. Well, as responsible adults perhaps we have to learn not to lose that child within us. I think I did for a long time, Cale," she said pensively, suddenly quite serious. Then Allison gave herself a good shake and turned to him with a laugh. "I think this is cause for a celebration. I've got a bottle of excellent wine back in my cabin. What do you say to a toast?"

"Last one back is a rotten egg!" He grinned, taking off at a brisk run that left her in his wake, her mouth agape.

"No fair, Cale Harding!" she called after him as she began to run. "You got a headstart!"

By the time Allison reached the door of her cabin, she was out of breath and bent over with a stitch in her side. She fell rather dramatically against Cale as he leaned against the door with his arms nonchalantly folded across his chest.

"Oh!" She groaned, gulping for air, "I think I left more than the spirit of childhood behind me."

"Out of shape, Miss Saunders?" he said, trying to breathe normally and almost succeeding.

"Perhaps," she murmured, taking in his efforts to disguise his own breathlessness. Allison raised one well-defined brow in his direction. "Am I to understand then, Mr. Harding, that your own rather heavy breathing is *not* due to our recent exertion, but some nameless passion on your part?" The inquiry was delivered in a saucy tone of voice. Allison knew she had him.

"My passion is anything but nameless, honey." Cale pulled her into his arms and swooped down to capture her mouth with his. As the kiss deepened, his hands slipped beneath her poncho, cupping her rounded bottom and pressing her tightly against him. When Cale finally raised his head again, he gave a disgruntled cough to hide the effect she had on him. "Now, about that wine . . ."

"Yes . . ." Allison said a little absently. "I think I could use a glass."

Tossing her poncho aside, Allison went on to the kitchen. She had the corkscrew inserted in the bottle before Cale made an appearance beside her.

"I'll do that if you'd like to get a towel to dry your hair," he suggested, giving her braid a playful tug. "You seem a mite bit wet, honey."

"My hair can wait for a moment," she replied. She yanked on the corkscrew, releasing the cork with a small pop. Allison looked up at Cale with a pleased expression on her face. "There," she said, quickly easing past him. "Now for the hair. I'm sure you know where to find the wineglasses," she called out over her shoulder.

When she returned with a towel wrapped turban-fashion around her head, Allison found Cale, soft music, and two glasses of wine waiting.

"That was quick," she commented, curling up on the opposite end of the sofa from him.

Cale politely handed her a glass and waited until she put

it to her lips before he spoke. "Some things are better done quickly, and then some things should be savored and lingered over . . . like a good wine," he said, touching his glass to hers.

Allison nearly choked at his innocent air. She had discovered in the past few weeks that Cale possessed a rather ribald sense of humor at times. He was a master of the double entendre.

"Then may all your *wines* be good ones," she said, with more than a suspicion of sarcasm in her voice.

"I only choose the best, sweetheart," murmured Cale, rolling his tongue around in his mouth as if he were testing the wine's bouquet.

"I'm sure you do," Allison muttered under her breath as he refilled her glass and then his own.

Setting her wine on the table at their feet, she removed the towel and began to undo her braid, running her fingers through the tangle of wet hair.

Cale reached out and plucked the towel from her lap. "Come on over here and I'll dry that for you," he said, twisting a lock of her hair around his finger.

Allison slid across the sofa until she was sitting within easy reach of him. Cale took the towel and began to rub her hair vigorously.

"Ouch!" she exclaimed when he inadvertently caught a tangle of hair in his hand.

"Sorry about that," he said apologetically. "I think I could do a better job of this if you were sitting below me." He looked around for a moment and spotted several throw pillows on the sofa. Cale tossed them into a pile at his feet. "Why don't you sit on those?" he suggested.

"All right," murmured Allison, slipping off the sofa

onto the stack of cushions. "I have a feeling you like a woman to be at your feet, anyway," she muttered under her breath, making sure it was just loud enough to be heard.

Cale renewed his task with a little more force than was absolutely necessary. "What did you say, sweetheart?" he asked in an innocent tone.

"Nothing, *sweetheart,*" she returned, gritting her teeth.

Cale took his time rubbing her hair to a state of near dryness, then he dropped the towel and began to massage her head and neck with his fingers. Allison resisted the allure of his hands on her flesh at first, but as the massage gradually transformed into a caress, she gave in to the seductive touch of his fingers.

"Oh, that feels good," she finally admitted, letting her head fall forward on her neck to give him access to her shoulders as well.

His hands seemed to possess magical qualities as they alternately massaged and caressed the muscles of her neck and shoulders. With slow, soothing strokes, he instinctively sought and found each point in need of comfort from her long day at the typewriter.

Allison could feel the tension and soreness fade under his touch, could feel a certain languor and a sense of complete relaxation spread through her body. Then as Cale's hands began to move in a more deliberate motion that languid feeling was gradually replaced by awareness, an awareness of what his touch could do to her. She could tell by the movement of his hands that Cale was not unaffected by the physical contact either. Her own breathing changed tempo as he ran his fingers halfway down her back and up again to her neck in light, caressing strokes.

147

He drew her back against his legs. "Your blouse is wet," he murmured, putting his hand on her shoulder with apparent casualness. "Perhaps you should take it off."

Allison sucked in her breath for a moment, then reached down and slowly undid first one button and then a second until the blouse hung open from neck to waist. She slipped it off her arms and laid it on the table, sitting there in only a scant lacy bra. Then she turned onto her knees, placed a hand on each of his muscular legs, and looked up at him with eyes that could kindle the coldest fire.

"You'll catch pneumonia in those wet clothes," she murmured in a softly seductive voice.

When Cale's hand went to the top button of his shirt, she impatiently pushed it out of the way and began to unbutton it herself. Each movement was deliberate and exaggerated as Allison undid the buttons down the front of his shirt, her eyes never leaving his face. When she reached the last button at his belt buckle, she paused for a moment with her hand on his abdomen and felt the small, barely perceptible shudder that passed down his body.

She grew more daring in her caresses, running her hand back and forth across the taut stomach and down the equally muscular thigh. Then she took a deep, steadying breath and boldly pressed her hand to the growing evidence of the effect her touch had on him, gently caressing him through the thick material of his jeans.

Cale exhaled her name on a trembling, husky breath and reached down and pulled her into his arms. "Oh, babe, do you have any idea of what you do to me?" he muttered against her mouth.

"I have a pretty good idea," she replied saucily, continuing to tease him with both her words and her caress.

Unable to contain himself any longer, Cale released a muffled groan, capturing both of her hands in one of his as he held them in front of her. The maneuver pressed her barely covered breasts together, their tips teasing the skin of her bare arms. He pulled her between his legs and drew her arms around his neck. Half-kneeling in front of him, Allison threw her head back as his lips sought the smoothness of her neck and shoulder, and lastly, the shadowy valley between her breasts.

His tongue flicked in and out like a seductive serpent as he manipulated first one nipple and then the other through the flimsy barrier of her bra. The red-rose peaks strained against the obstacle between them and the source of their exquisite pleasure, swelling against the tip of his audacious, darting tongue. He nipped one hardened nipple and then the other in turn, leaving a small damp spot in the center of her breasts, which only served more clearly to outline their aroused state.

With Cale's arms entwined about her waist for support, Allison pulled back for a moment and slowly slipped first one strap and then the other down her shoulders. His eyes, dark with unspoken desire, grew even darker and more intense as she released the last hook.

No longer content simply to look on, Cale drew one hand from her waist to cover a rosy mound. He gently touched and caressed and molded her with his palm until she yearned for even greater pleasures.

With a low moan, Allison pushed herself against his chest and forced his head back with the force of her mouth on his, covering it in a kiss that was asking and giving at

149

the same instant. She teased his lips and tongue and teeth with her own pink, probing tongue, then drove deeper into his mouth with a mounting need and excitement, spurred on by the touch of his bare skin rubbing against her own.

Cale seized the two rounded halves of her bottom in his hands and urged her even closer to the center of their passionate need. Then he reluctantly pulled his mouth from hers and went in search of further erotic pleasures, nibbling a sensuous path along her arm to take one exposed nipple into his mouth.

At his touch, Allison groaned her need aloud, a need that only he could satisfy. "Yes, oh, Cale, yes!"

Leaving no stimulation untried, he soon had them both on the edge of physical torment. His fingers found the button at the top of her jeans and eased it and the zipper away from her flesh. He stood her before him, keeping her between his legs, and drew the material down over her hips, followed by the pair of lacy panties beneath. Allison stepped away from her discarded clothing and turned to reciprocate, reaching for the buckle at his waist. She tugged the jeans from his legs as he sat there, his eyes feasting on the sight of her nude body damp with perspiration from her efforts.

Then they stood before each other as man and woman. Cale drew her back down to him, this time his legs between hers as he settled her astride his hips. Allison merged with him in the slow, sensual movements that would take them both on that final exquisite journey to the stars.

She felt her own passion building with a force she had never known before. She cried out as he grasped her breasts in his hands and raised them to his lips. His mouth

150

covered one while his fingertips caressed the other, as she tried and sometimes failed to keep pace with the rhythm of their lovemaking.

Cale gripped her fiercely by the hips as they reached together for that glorious moment when all else stood suspended but the passionate pleasure they gave to the other. They hurried on now to that ultimate climax that would release them from this exquisite torment, a mutual cry surfacing from their lips as they met that moment as one.

Allison's head fell to his shoulder as she wrapped her arms about his neck and held him close. There were no words to express what had taken place between them and so they sat there, clinging to each other in the aftermath of their loving.

Countless minutes passed unheeded. When Allison finally roused herself and started to move away, Cale stopped her with a glance filled with need. He clasped their bodies together and swept her beneath him onto the length of the sofa. Without once losing their oneness, he began anew to kiss her mouth and nose and the tips of her fully aroused breasts.

"Cale?" A single word expressed her bewilderment as she gazed up at him with eyes still clouded with the passion just passed.

"That was just the beginning, babe, not the end," he muttered, kissing her with a long, lingering kiss, infinite in its tenderness.

Gentle hands stroked the smooth length of her body as though he wanted nothing more than to be with her like this for the rest of their lives, as though they had all the time in the world to savor and appreciate each other as a man and a woman.

As he continued to caress and kiss each and every point of pleasure, she sensed his desire building again, rising from the ashes of their passion.

Cale teased and cajoled her into an even greater display of passion, his own need igniting the very essence of her. Then in a tremendous burst of energy, he raised himself on his elbows and moved with a force and power that left her beautifully mindless in a matter of seconds. She realized he had every intention of taking her on the erotic journey of her life.

He gave her pleasure after pleasure until she was certain she would surely die here in his arms and not care if she did. Allison cried out his name in a voice that proved he had accomplished his goal. And then—when she knew she could take no more, that heaven was never meant to be within the grasp of mere mortals—Cale took a heaving breath of air and joined her on that last journey they took together.

He cried out her name, a sheen of perspiration covering them both, as he gently eased himself down atop her. They lay there, satiated in mind and spirit and body, holding each other, not caring or daring to speak.

When Allison finally stirred from the exhausted sleep that followed, she realized they were still there, entwined on the sofa. She turned her head to look at the man at her side, her eyes filled with a sense of awe and wonder and love.

It was then she knew her worst fear. Dear God, she was in love with Cale! With all that she was, with her heart and soul and body, she worshipped him. He was everything she had ever dreamed of and more. Cale was friend and lover, and she wanted him—not for the moment, not even for a matter of weeks—but for the rest of her life.

He slept on in the exhaustive aftermath of their love-making, oblivious to the discovery she had made, totally unaware of the joy and torment that rent her heart from her body as it became totally and completely his for the asking. Allison reached out and stroked his face as she acknowledged in the deepest recesses of her heart that she loved him as she had never thought she could love anyone.

Cale's eyes flickered open at last. He remained motionless, staring into her eyes with a warmth and tenderness that touched her as nothing else could have at that moment.

"It's—" His voice broke on a husky note. "It's never been like that for me," he said, with intense satisfaction.

"Nor for me," Allison murmured, letting out a sigh. She took a deep breath and finished almost hopefully, "I love you, Cale."

An expression flitted across his features that she could put no name to. It was gone before it had begun. Cale reached out a lazy hand and touched her lips with his finger. Yet the words she wanted to hear were not forthcoming. When the silence stretched unnaturally into one long minute after another, she began to wonder if he had heard her. Perhaps she had only imagined saying the words aloud.

"I . . . I don't know how it happened, but, dear God, I love you, Cale Harding," she repeated through the gradually subsiding thunder of her heart.

Cale was very quiet. Then he caught his breath with

153

what sounded like a groan. "I heard you, honey," he finally said, his own voice denying all emotion.

Allison felt his withdrawal from her more in spirit than in any physical sense. And then she knew there was a fear worse than loving Cale—that was to love him without being loved in return.

"I would like to get up now," she said rigidly, gesturing toward the masculine leg that had her own pinned beneath it.

Cale looked faintly puzzled for a moment. "Allison—"

"Please, just let me get up," she repeated without anger, but with a kind of cold finality in her voice. "My back hurts," she added for good measure. Although the pain was real, it was not in her back, but rather in her heart.

But the lie served its purpose. Cale finally assented and moved his leg. Allison slipped off the sofa and without stopping to pick up her discarded clothing or even once looking back, she walked out of the room.

The tears did not start until she had reached the safety of her bedroom. And then they came hot and heavy and filled with bitterness.

CHAPTER EIGHT

"Allison."

At the sound of Cale's voice outside the bedroom door, she quickly raised her head from the pillow and reached for a tissue from the box on the bedside table. Wiping her face, she discreetly gave a little blow. She was half off the bed when the door unceremoniously flew open and hit the wall behind it with a resounding crack.

Cale stood framed in the doorway, an imposing figure, standing tall in the light. Allison noted, almost with embarrassment, that he was once more wearing the jeans she had eagerly removed in the heat of their passion.

In the space of one hour how had she gone from being the happiest of women to the most miserable? If only she didn't love him. If only he loved her. Cale had once told her there were no guarantees. She just hadn't realized how true that was until the past few minutes.

"Dammit, Allison." He swore in a voice that did not entirely disguise his impatience. "I never meant to hurt you," he stated, an edge of steel underlining each word.

She got up without speaking and quickly drew on her robe, suddenly finding her nudity an embarrassment. Then she turned to him, knowing she could not hide the fact that she had been crying, scornful of the sympathy in his eyes.

"Have you ever really loved anyone in your entire life?" she asked, unable to disguise her hurt and anger.

"Please, Allison, don't do this to us," he said in the softest tone she had ever heard him use. "We've got something great going for us."

"Yes." She laughed raggedly. "A great sexual relationship. But then life is more than sex, isn't it, Cale?"

"We both know that," he said with a disparaging click of his tongue. "But it is the basis for any good relationship. Don't kid yourself."

"Perhaps it's the basis, but there has to be more than just jumping into bed with each other," she returned, even as she admitted to herself that they had far more than that. Still, she needed, wanted, more than Cale was apparently willing or able to give.

"You have to understand, dammit!" he went on. "You're expecting something from me that I can't give you."

"Then you're admitting you are incapable of giving love," she said, her voice bruised with pain. "And I thought *I* was some kind of emotional cripple because I felt incapable of making a commitment to anyone or anything." She snorted. "Well, compared to you, Cale Harding, I'm the picture of mental health."

"Don't judge what you can't understand, Allison," he replied, enunciating each word as if it were a dagger.

"Oh, yes, how could I presume to judge the great Christian Trent?" she said bitterly, fighting back the tears of anger.

"Dammit! That's just what I mean." Cale jumped on

156

her, his voice rising in a dark rage. "For the last time, I am not Christian Trent! I'm Cale Harding and I am a man, a flesh-and-blood man just like any other. I thought you of all people would understand that."

He might be flesh and blood, Allison thought to herself, but he was definitely not like any other man, not for her. She knew now that she loved him desperately, but she would never beg him for his love when he had none to give.

She gave a great sigh and tried to calm herself. "I . . . I do understand, at least most of the time," she admitted in a soft, defeated tone. "I spoke in anger, Cale. We all say things in anger we don't mean. But you must understand, too, that I want things out of life that I know I can't have with you. I want a real home, not some hotel suite. I want routine and normalcy and friends and three mornings a week working out at the Y. You move from place to place with no schedule, no friends, no life beyond your writing. That might be all right for a brief affair. I thought I could handle our relationship knowing that's all it was . . . but I can't anymore." She spoke in a barely audible voice. "I want more, Cale, so much more."

"I'm giving you all that I can, Allison," he said in an equally soft voice. "This is my life-style whether you like it or not. I've been on my own for most of my life. I had to be in the beginning, and now I want to be. I warned you that writing was a solitary life. It doesn't leave much room for anything else."

She looked up at him with a faint light of hope still in her eyes. "But other people write and they have homes and wives and children and a dog and a station wagon," she pointed out.

157

"That's not my style, babe. I honestly thought you understood that from the beginning. There are no strings in my life, Allison. That's the way it must be for me."

"No strings," she repeated thoughtfully, realizing that was exactly what she had always assumed she wanted for herself—at least until she met this man. But it wasn't true anymore. She knew now that there was no such thing as living without strings. Even Cale had them if he looked closely enough. It was suddenly clear to her as it had never been before. She felt calmer, if sadder, for the knowing. Someday Cale would realize too, but it would not be in time to help her.

"Well, it was fun while it lasted." Allison made an attempt at humor and failed.

"What do you mean, while it lasted?" Cale said in a brusque tone, taking another step into the room.

"As you said yourself, we both knew from the start that all of this was purely temporary." She gestured with her hand at their immediate surroundings. "We gave ourselves the chance we said we would, and now it's over," she announced with a shrug. "I called my family and several of my close friends this morning and told them I would be back in New York within the week." Allison vowed to make those calls the minute he was gone. "It's the first week of August already and the new Broadway season and the opera will be opening next month." Did he detect the tremor in her voice? She forced herself to continue. "I wouldn't dream of missing that.

"And I have some connections with an editor at one of the major magazines. She would like me to bring in some of my work and review what I've been doing this summer. I have so many things to get done in the next few weeks.

I can't do them stuck up here in the woods, now can I?" She concluded with a face-saving smile.

Allison was rather proud of her speech, impromptu as it was. She was determined to end this affair with at least part of her dignity and self-respect intact.

Cale looked at her with an expression of skepticism and perhaps even surprise on his face. "You're leaving?"

"I really do think it's time," Allison replied with as much nonchalance as she could muster. "Don't think it hasn't been wonderful being here with you, because it has been." She nearly stumbled over that and said too much. "But just as your career must come first with you, so mine must with me. It's the chance I've always promised myself, Cale, and I won't give it up for anything or anyone. You of all people should understand that." Allison knew that was the strongest argument in her defense.

"I suppose I understand," Cale finally muttered, not looking at all pleased. His career demanded that he have a quiet place in which to work on his new book and hers required that she return to New York. That left little room for discussion or compromise.

"Somehow I knew you would, professional that you are through and through," Allison stated, with a funny little grimace. It wasn't entirely meant as a compliment. "I just hope you don't wake up one day and realize that all you really know of life is what you write about it. That somehow along the way you have forgotten to live it as well," she murmured with sad sincerity. "We all need other people, Cale—even you do, in the end." She had said too much, she knew that, but somehow the words needed to be said for their own sake.

"I've gotten along on my own without anyone else for

nearly fifteen years," he said quickly, almost harshly. "So spare me the lectures on how we all need other people, if you don't mind. There's only one person anyone can count on when it comes right down to it, honey, and that's himself."

"I'm sure you believe that," she murmured, knowing her defeat was complete and irrevocable. She wasn't going to change the attitudes of a lifetime with a few clever statements, she saw that now. Allison felt as if some part of herself and Cale had already said their farewells. It was truly over.

"When are you planning to leave?" Cale asked reluctantly.

"I see no reason to delay the inevitable. I have my collection of short stories completed"—another lie passed her lips—"and I'm a little tired of parading around in jeans and cheap cotton shirts," she added, with a glance to her closet. "It will feel good to wear decent clothes again." She hoped Cale was buying everything she said, though she cringed inwardly at the image she was projecting of herself. "I can't wait to go out to a decent restaurant and see the new fashions for fall," she stated, injecting a note of enthusiasm into her voice that was as phony as her smile.

Allison wanted to shout at him that none of it made any difference if he didn't love her, but her sense of self-preservation stepped in to keep her from making a complete fool of herself.

"I thought you had changed somehow while you were up here," Cale said with just the slightest hint of disgust in his voice. "But I see that underneath it all you are still the same silly, superficial woman you always were."

That was unnecessarily cruel. Allison found herself hating him just a little, her hand itching to wipe the smirk off his face.

"Don't you ever call me a silly, superficial woman," she rasped with barely controlled fury. "Don't you ever dare! It's arrogant and chauvinistic and patronizing—and beneath the intelligence and dignity of a man like yourself." She shook from head to toe with emotion.

Cale ran his hand through his hair in a gesture of frustration. "I think there's a compliment somewhere in that chewing out, but I'll be damned if I can figure out where," he admitted, confounded.

Allison nearly laughed and realized that she still could. Dear God, she could still laugh. She hoped she remembered this moment in the weeks and months to come. She had the strongest premonition that she would need to recall this moment for the sake of her sanity.

"Oh, hell, I apologize for calling you a silly woman," Cale muttered, swearing under his breath. Then he looked up at her, his eyes lined with something akin to pain. "I don't want you to go, Allison." It was as close to asking her to stay as he would get. She knew that somehow.

"I see no other alternative, do you?" She looked him straight in the eyes.

"You could always stay . . ." he finally said in a rough voice.

"You could always come to New York with me," she countered uncompromisingly.

The irreconcilability of their situation left them both silent and bereft. They stood gazing at each other across the small bedroom, both realizing that he would stay and she would go. It was the only way for them.

"You never did tell me when you're planning to leave," Cale reminded her, looking vaguely out the window, his hands stuffed in the pockets of his jeans.

Allison felt as if she were poised on the edge of a great chasm, not wanting to move in either direction, but knowing she must. She had told Cale that she loved him and he had made no answering reply. She told him she was leaving and he asked when.

"I . . . ah, I have to get back to Dartmouth somehow and pick up my car, and then it's going to be several days of hard driving back to New York. If I want to be home by next week then I need to be on my way by tomorrow," she decided on the spur of the moment.

"Tomorrow!" That brought Cale's head around with a jerk.

"There's no reason for me to stay here any longer, Cale," she stated, this time without a spark of hope in her voice.

"Then tonight is our last night together," he murmured, as if that had some special meaning.

Allison looked at him and knew in her heart that if she allowed him to make love to her again all her resolve to leave would melt under his expert touch. She dared not take that chance. Loving him as she did, it would be torture to hold him, to love him, knowing all the while that it would have to last her a lifetime.

"No!" The word seemed to pop out of her mouth of its own volition.

"No?" Cale looked at her, puzzled.

"No, tonight is not our last night together," Allison said in a tone that held no compromise. "Last night was our last night together." She knew he understood the meaning behind her words. This afternoon had been the experience of a lifetime, but she had no intentions of repeating it. She might go a little weak in the knees at the mere sight of this man, but she was no masochist. What was that quotation? If it must be done, then it was better done quickly? That was a paraphrase, but the meaning was the same. There would be no long, drawn-out good-byes for her and Cale.

"Well, it's not night yet," Cale said in a brusque, dry voice as he headed straight for her and pulled her into his arms. "Say what you will, lady, you can't tell me you don't want me and make me believe it!" he growled, driving his mouth down on hers, his teeth cutting into her lip.

Oh, God, she wanted to love him and have him love her, but never like this—not out of anger, not with the intent to inflict pain on each other. And yet, even in pain, Allison felt herself responding to him, to the mouth that was no longer cruel, to the roughness that had become a caress. She wrapped her arms around him, her kiss, her touch, telling him that she loved him.

Cale pushed her away from him, his breathing heavy and labored. He stared at her with eyes dark and disturbed. "I think I could have accepted your hate, Allison. It's your love I can't tolerate." His hands dropped to his sides in defeat. "I'll drive you back to Dartmouth myself in the morning," he said in a flat tone.

She wanted to object, but realized it was her only way out of these mountains. The idea of spending several hours in the close confines of the Bronco with Cale was painful, but not nearly as painful as staying on here at the colony until she could manage to arrange for some other means of transportation.

"All right, Cale," she finally agreed, telling herself it

would all be over in a few hours. "I would like to leave as early as possible."

Cale gave her a look that no doubt replaced a thousand words, but in her present state of mind Allison couldn't decipher it.

"Be ready at eight sharp," he said cold-bloodedly, then turned on his heel and left the room.

She waited until she could no longer hear him moving about the cabin before she left the haven of her bedroom. His clothes were gone and he was, too. Only the half-empty wineglasses on the table remained as proof that he had even been there. That and the pain in Allison's heart as she picked up the glasses and carried them to the kitchen.

With only half-conscious movements, she began the arduous task of packing her belongings and putting the cabin to rights. She was almost grateful for the busy work. At least, it kept her from completely falling to pieces. There would always be time for that, she told herself with a wry smile.

Later that evening, when she thought she could talk without breaking down, she put a call through to her parents and informed them of her intention to return to New York. Her mother sensed that something was wrong, but Allison pleaded exhaustion as the reason for the life-lessness in her voice. Her mother wisely dropped the subject. It was nearly two o'clock when Allison crawled into bed, truly exhausted this time.

She was waiting on the front stoop of the cabin, her suitcases and belongings stacked beside her, when Cale drove up in the Bronco on the stroke of eight. As a subtle indication she was indeed returning to her normal life-style, Allison had chosen to wear one of her chicest, most expensive outfits for the first leg of the long journey home.

With a perfunctory nod of his head, Cale got out of the vehicle and picked up a suitcase. "Is that everything?" he finally said as they loaded what appeared to be the last of her luggage in the back of the Bronco.

"Yes, thank you," she replied in the same stilted, too-polite tone. She had not been able to bring herself to say good morning to him. It wasn't a good morning for either of them.

Apparently, it had not been a good night either, Allison thought, noting the strain lines around Cale's eyes and the dark circles beneath them. She did not need to look in a mirror to know her own were just as strained and smudged, although makeup could do wonders for a woman.

Once they were both seated in the truck, Cale turned to her with a tight-lipped expression. "Are you sure this is what you want to do?" He gave her a quick, penetrating look.

"Yes," she finally replied, averting her eyes.

His voice grew softer, almost caressing. "I may not be able to say the things you need to hear, Allison, but you know that I want you."

Men had always *wanted* her. That wasn't what she needed to hear from this man, this one special man. She wanted him to say he loved her, he needed her, he wanted to spend the rest of his life with her. She couldn't settle for less, and she wouldn't!

Groping to recover her inner balance, Allison grated, "Yes, I know. But it just wouldn't work now, don't you see?" Fatigue and strain had shorn her of her defenses.

Cale stared straight ahead of him, his hands gripping the steering wheel until the knuckles were white. "At least try to appreciate the fact that I've always been honest with you. I could have taken advantage of the situation and lied to you," he pointed out in his own defense.

"You have always been honest with me," Allison repeated nearly verbatim. A lot of good it did her. For a moment, she almost wished he had lied to her. At least that way she would have his words of love to treasure in her heart, even if they weren't true. But she knew if he had, the parting would have been even more hurtful and bitter.

"You were right about one thing," Cale said, slamming the vehicle into gear. "I have never really been in love. I'm not sure love even exists," he concluded so softly she wasn't certain she had heard him correctly.

Allison turned her head and stared out the window, seeing the cabins disappear around the bend in the road as they drove away. She would always remember the two weeks she had spent in this place—the source of her greatest joy and her lasting sorrow.

The drive to Hanover was made in complete silence. Cale paid undivided attention to his driving, and Allison stayed deep in her own thoughts.

If only she had not fallen in love with this man, she cried to herself. They could have spent the summer together with no strings, no commitment, and no lasting regrets when they parted. But she knew herself well enough to realize that sex and love went hand-in-hand for a woman like her. She was incapable of separating the two, despite current attitudes to the contrary.

Cale wanted her, and if she had been able to accept him

on that basis, their affair could have continued indefinitely. But she cared too much for Cale Harding and for herself to stay in a relationship where the love was one-sided. Both people had to be equally involved, equally committed, if it were not to turn into a bitter experience in the end.

She had mistaken his thoughtfulness, his tenderness, as a possibility of far more. It had simply not worked out that way. She had unknowingly gambled and knowingly lost. Love had crept up on her and given her the surprise of her life. She had never been one to like surprises, she acknowledged to herself.

Allison held on to herself with an iron grip, fearing if she relaxed for even a moment, she would say or do something to her everlasting regret. She couldn't force Cale to love her. She could not make him need her. He truly believed he didn't need or love anyone.

If only it had been another woman. She would have been almost relieved. At least that was something she could have understood, that she could have fought. But how did she fight an enemy that existed inside the man she loved?

The miles and the minutes passed, if all too slowly, and they finally arrived back in the town of Hanover. Cale drove straight to the garage where they had stored her car and insisted on dealing with the owner himself, ordering Allison to remain in the Bronco.

She watched as he concluded the business of paying the man in charge, her eyes not missing one look, one move, Cale made. The memories she stored up now would have to last her for all the lonely nights ahead.

Then Cale returned and began to unload her luggage

and transfer it piece by piece to her Porsche. Allison got out of the Bronco and carried some of the smaller bags herself. Then everything was ready. There was no reason to delay her departure. The moment had come when she must say good-bye to this man and get in her car and drive away.

Oh, dear God! How could she turn her back and simply walk out of his life? She silently intoned a plea for courage, knowing that to delay the inevitable would not make it any less difficult.

Cale opened the door on the driver's side and gave her a hand into the Porsche. Then he leaned his head into the open window and briefly, softly, touched his lips to hers.

"Take care of yourself, Allison Saunders," he whispered, placing a finger to her mouth. "If I ever thought I could love someone, that someone would be you."

Then Cale stepped away from the car and raised his hand in salute.

Allison put the car into gear and pulled away from the garage, willing herself not to look in the rear-view mirror, knowing she would crumble if she saw Cale's tall form standing there watching her drive away. As it was, she died a little more inside with each mile of the road traveled.

She was just on the outskirts of town when she pulled off the highway and buried her head in her arms, leaning on the steering wheel for support. She gave in to the tears that had been threatening her vision for the past few miles. She cried long and hard until she felt dead inside.

CHAPTER NINE

Clad only in her underthings, with her hands resting on her hips, Allison stood in the center of the walk-in closet, intently studying the rack of dresses in front of her. She wanted something feminine, but not excessively frilly to wear for her dinner date tonight.

The yellow chiffon would have to go, she mused. It just wasn't her style anymore. There was a secondhand designer shop on Third Avenue that wouldn't mind getting their hands on it. And she understood the money went for a good cause.

She finally decided on the raspberry bouclé knit and took it from the rack and hung it on the back of the door. She wanted to look nice for her evening with Roger, but after all they had known each other since she was a girl in French braids and braces. Roger had known her too long to be impressed by anything she might do to herself. Besides, it wasn't like that between Roger Shelley and her.

Allison had spent the past month since returning home from New Hampshire writing and thinking, rarely leaving her apartment. In fact, this was the first time she had gone out since her return. She had looked up a friend at one of the major magazines the first week back, and they were

169

looking at three of her stories right now. Their response had been most encouraging.

She strolled into her bedroom, the raspberry knit in hand, and carefully laid it out on the bed. It was a small but luxurious room, furnished in white wicker and pale-peach accents. A feminine bedroom, one she had decorated herself. She was lucky to have the walk-in closet. They were a rarity in New York, where space was always at a premium.

Allison went into the living room, scarcely noticing the sophisticated blend of blues and browns and the select accent pieces she had acquired over the years. There were numerous oils on the walls, all originals done by up-and-coming East Coast artists, and even a few pieces of weaving and sculpture to add to the room's interest.

The kitchen and dining room were directly off the living room and there was a half bath and storage pantry in the rear. That was the extent of Allison's apartment, but it was quite spacious by New York standards.

She poured herself a glass of orange juice and sipped it as she returned to the bedroom to get dressed, thinking of Roger's timely call a few days before. It was almost as if he had known that she needed to pick up the pieces of her life and get on with it. She was tired of being cooped up within the four walls of her apartment. It was time she started seeing old friends again.

Allison admitted—at least to herself—that never a day or a night went by that she didn't think of Cale Harding. The pain and the embarrassment were still there, but she had stopped crying herself to sleep. And she had started eating properly once she realized she had dropped five pounds she could ill afford to lose.

She had told no one about Cale or their affair, not even her best friend, Marilyn. That was a part of her life that would always remain private. She didn't think she could bear to put it into words. Somehow it would all come out sounding rather sordid, and it had been anything but that.

There had been no word from Cale, not that Allison had expected to hear from him. She had known full well when she walked out that that would be the end of it. It was quite clear to her now that Cale had meant more to her than she ever had to him. That was the problem in a one-sided love affair, the love was all on one side.

She knew it would take far longer than a month for the love she felt to settle somewhere in the back of her heart. There it would lie for the rest of her life as a reminder of Cale and what they had shared that summer. She comforted herself with the knowledge that surely the passage of time would relieve the awful pain of loving him.

Allison gave her hair a good brushing and swept it back on either side, securing it with combs. She applied a light rub of blush and a touch of lip gloss. Since her return from the New Hampshire mountains, she had discovered a number of changes in herself, even in the way she wanted to look and feel about herself. She took less time with her appearance, instead trying to concentrate on the person she was on the inside.

Her family and the few friends she had seen since she got back had noticed the difference in her immediately. It was subtle, but to people who knew Allison well, it was unmistakable. She was quieter, more ready to listen than to talk, less concerned with appearances. Allison liked to think that knowing and loving Cale had added a depth to her character that made her a more empathetic human being.

She was ready a good half hour before Roger was due to arrive. She thought about the dear friend she had known since childhood. Roger Shelley was a successful New York lawyer now, but he had had his share of bad times, too. He had gone through a disastrous marriage a few years back. Now, whenever he or Allison were between romantic interests or simply wanted an evening out with a good friend who was sure to understand, they would give the other a call.

She supposed Roger had heard through the grapevine that she had spent most of the summer in New Hampshire. She wondered if he would notice the changes she felt in herself. Even if he did, he was the kind of friend who would not remark about them unkindly.

Allison was sitting in the living room, reading a copy of that day's *Wall Street Journal,* when the buzzer sounded at her door. She got up and returned the buzz, unlocking the front entryway, thinking Roger, as usual, was fifteen minutes early.

Then there followed a soft knock at her door, the brass knocker falling twice in quick succession. Knowing what a pleasure it always was to see her old friend, Allison felt a smile light her face as she answered the door.

"Roger—" She felt the smile freeze on her features. It wasn't Roger Shelley standing there, but the tall, brooding figure of Cale Harding!

She noted the quick almost scowling frown he gave her.

"Hello, Allison," he said, after the briefest of pauses.

"Hello, Cale," she replied in a polite, impersonal tone. She made no move, stunned by his unexpected appearance

172

and preoccupied with not letting him see what the sight of him was doing to her composure.

"I have to talk to you, Allison," he announced, barging past her into the room beyond. "Very nice, very you," he commented, then turned again to face her, the decor of her apartment instantly dismissed from his mind.

"I'm expecting someone in a few minutes, Cale," Allison stated, determined to assert herself. "Why don't you give me a call in the morning and we'll arrange to meet somewhere." Her hand still clasped the door knob.

"Who's Roger?" Cale inquired, apparently noticing for the first time that she was dressed to go out.

"*That* is none of your business," replied Allison, firmly but not impolitely. "Now, I really must ask you to leave before he gets here." She dismissed him with a gesture directed toward the still-open door.

"Not so fast, sweetheart," he drawled, plunking himself down on her sofa. "I drove like a madman all the way from New Hampshire to talk to you and talk to you I will."

"We can talk tomorrow, Cale," she repeated, her patience starting to leave, even though she was curious. She was damned if she would allow this man to barge back into her life as though nothing had happened! She had been trying to put him out of her mind for a whole month. It wasn't fair that he should unwittingly shatter in a matter of a few minutes what little peace of mind she had managed to attain She would talk to him when and where she pleased, if at all. There was no room in her heart to forgive and forget, not yet. "I want you out of my apartment now," Allison went on. "I did not invite you here,

173

and I have a date arriving at any time. I want you gone before he gets here," she said, facing him squarely.

The door buzzer sounded again. With a sinking feeling that a confrontation was now impossible to avoid, Allison returned the buzz.

"It looks like it's too late now," Cale intoned, quite satisfied with himself. "You'll just have to introduce me to Mr. Right after all." He sat back against the cushions and folded his arms across his chest.

Allison started to say that Roger was not Mr. Right and then thought better of it. Let Cale think what he might, she growled to herself as she went to answer the door for the second time.

"Hello, Roger." She greeted him enthusiastically, holding out both of her hands to the handsome blond framed in the doorway.

"Allison, honey. You look stunning, as always," purred the smooth, sophisticated man as he took her hands in his and placed a warm kiss on her lips. "In fact, I don't think I've ever seen you looking better, my love," he murmured in a suggestive undertone.

Roger had a line a mile long, but he could do wonders for a woman's ego. It never took him more than a few seconds to size up any situation and respond accordingly. Allison supposed it was the lawyer in him. When Roger finally realized there was another man in the room, he didn't lose his stride, even for a split second.

"Please, come in, Roger. This is . . ." She hesitated for a moment, wondering how she should introduce the dark, scowling man sprawled on her sofa. "This is an old student of mine from the days at Park Academy, Cale Harding," she said, knowing that was the last thing Cale would expect her to say.

"It's a pleasure meeting you, Mr. Harding," Roger said congenially, extending his hand.

His action forced Cale to his feet. As he returned the handshake, the contrast between the two was all the more emphatic. There was Roger with his Ivy League good looks and smooth, sophisticated manner, dressed in a tailor-made suit that befit his station in life. And there was Cale Harding—big and muscular, his lean hips and long legs attired in a pair of jeans that had seen better days. Roger was a tall man, but Cale got the better of him by several inches. The contrast between the two men would have been startling, if it had not been so ludicrous.

"Cale, this is an old and dear friend of mine, Roger Shelley," Allison murmured, finishing the formalities.

"So you were one of Allison's students," Roger said politely, making himself at home in one of the overstuffed armchairs.

"I was a long time ago," Cale remarked. "Actually, Allison and I spent the summer together in New Hampshire."

While Roger managed to assimilate this piece of information without so much as batting an eyelash, Allison felt herself blush at the insinuation behind Cale's declaration.

She decided then and there to give as good as she got. "Cale is better known by his professional name," she began, seeing the warning light go on in the big man's eyes. "He writes under the name Christian Trent." There! She had done it. And Cale deserved it too.

"Really." Roger was impressed, and Roger rarely was. "I must admit I'm a fan, Mr. Hard . . . *Trent.* It is a

175

pleasure meeting you. I assume you were also at the writers' workshop Allison attended at Dartmouth."

"I was at Dartmouth doing research when I ran into Allison," Cale explained, explanations rarely coming from him. "What do you do, Mr. Shelley?" he inquired with a politeness as phony as the smile pasted on his face.

"I'm an attorney," Roger answered modestly.

"One of the most highly respected attorneys in New York," Allison added, deliberately placing a hand on Roger's shoulder.

Why didn't Cale take the hint and leave? she wondered, wishing she had followed Roger's initial suggestion to go out a half hour earlier. Cale was up to something and whatever he had up his sleeve, she had a strange feeling she wasn't going to like it.

"I've driven all the way from New Hampshire today to see Allison," Cale began. "So I'm sure you'll understand why she can't go out with you tonight."

"Cale!" Allison's mouth dropped open in astonishment. "I have no intention of canceling my dinner date. How dare you come in here and try to run my life!" she sputtered angrily, seeing red.

"All right, if you won't cancel, then I'll just stay put until you get back," he drawled, slipping off his shoes and making himself right at home, even to the point of putting his feet up on her sofa.

"This has gone far enough, Cale," she said through thin lips. "Take your lousy feet off my sofa and get out of here this minute."

"Now, sweetheart, there's no reason to be embarrassed. I'm sure Roger understands things like a lovers' quarrel," he murmured, watching with delight as her face flushed a bright crimson.

"We are not lovers, and we are not going to have a quarrel because you are on your way out that door, Mr. Harding." She gestured angrily. It made her all the angrier when she saw Cale's lips twitch in an effort not to smile.

"But we were lovers, and we did have a quarrel," he pointed out ruthlessly. "Now, why put Mr. Shelley in what has to be an extremely awkward position by insisting that he stay? We have to talk tonight, Allison. This won't wait until morning. You can either go out with Roger and then come back here to face the music, or you can be sensible and let Roger be on his way, and we can have that talk now." He spoke as if he were being so reasonable. And Allison only wanted to strangle him, which was not reasonable at all.

Roger had been silent until now, but he cleared his throat to remind the combatants that there was a third party present and rose to his feet.

"I can't say I admire your tactics, Mr. Harding, but it seems that you and Allison have a great deal to say to each other that would be better said in private."

"Oh, Roger, please don't go. I can't tell you how sorry I am about all of this," Allison murmured, crestfallen.

"I'll take a rain check on that dinner, honey. I think the evening would have gone rather poorly under the circumstances, don't you agree?"

"Yes, I suppose it would have at that," she assented reluctantly.

Roger turned back for a moment to the man on the sofa. "I'm not certain I can say it was a pleasure, Mr. Harding. But remember this—if you do anything to hurt Allison, you will have me to answer to," he stated in his most intimidating courtroom manner. "Walk me to the door, Allison," he said, taking her elbow in his hand. "If you need me for any reason, you know where to call," he added under his breath. "And good luck, honey. I'd say you're going to need it." Then Roger opened the door and with a light peck to her cheek was gone.

Allison slowly closed the door after him, leaning her cheek against it momentarily for support. Then she straightened her shoulders and turned back into the room to face the man who waited there.

"Just because Roger decided to leave, don't get any ideas that you're staying," she fumed. "You can put your shoes on now and follow him right out that door. After what you have just done, I wouldn't talk to you tonight or any night!"

"Contrary to what you're thinking, I'm not proud of what I had to do just now," Cale confessed as he sat up and buried his head in his hands. The sudden change in his expression was startling.

"Then why in the world did you do it? You were abominably rude to one of my oldest and dearest friends. I don't think I can ever forgive you for that," Allison said in a voice that shook with emotion.

Cale raised his head and looked her straight in the eyes. "I suppose I did it out of desperation and jealousy. And I need your forgiveness for far more than being rude to a friend of yours, Allison."

"I . . . I don't want to have this conversation, Cale," she replied, her hands making little nervous gestures. "I meant it when I said I expect you to put on your shoes and get out of here." She retraced her steps to the door and

178

stood sentry there, as though she fully expected him to comply with her wishes.

"Dammit! I can't leave without—" His voice broke off on the last word.

Allison looked back at him with a puzzled expression on her face. There was the strangest light in Cale's eyes. They were shiny and rather bright—too bright. Dear God, those couldn't possibly be tears in his eyes, not Cale Harding. She doubted he had shed a tear over anything since he was a boy.

She watched without saying a word as he rose to his feet and stood gazing out the window of her apartment. His profile was outlined against the backdrop of soft drapes and Manhattan skyline. There was the familiar jutting chin and well-shaped nose, but she thought there was also a vulnerability about him she had not seen before. Cale vulnerable? She must be imagining things.

Allison moved away from the door and came to a stop a few feet from him. "Why did you come here tonight, Cale?"

He spoke without turning to look at her. "Do you think I could have a drink?"

She shrugged her shoulders in a gesture he failed to see. "I could make some coffee."

"I was thinking of something a little stronger than coffee," he replied in a low mocking tone.

"There's some Scotch in the kitchen," she finally said, realizing she could use a drink herself. It seemed they were going to have that talk tonight whether she liked it or not. "Do you want that with water or on the rocks?" she asked, almost by rote.

Cale turned and regarded her for some seconds before he answered. "On the rocks, please."

Allison did an about-face and walked out of the room, not realizing until she reached the kitchen how badly she was trembling. She leaned her forehead against the refrigerator door for a moment, grateful for its smooth, cool surface. She had to make it through this night without breaking down. She would not allow Cale to see her crying, she promised herself.

"Allison, is everything all right?" came the deep masculine voice behind her. "Are you feeling sick?"

She quickly straightened up, giving a covert swipe to the tears on her cheeks, making sure she did not turn her head toward him. "I'm fine, Cale," she managed to reassure him in a near-normal tone. "I was feeling a little lightheaded, that's all. I'm all right now. I haven't eaten since this morning and thanks to you, I missed my dinner," she added with biting sarcasm.

"I haven't eaten all day either," he commented, patting the lean, taut stomach above his beltline. "Why don't I call out and have something delivered?"

Allison swung around and bumped into the steel wall of his chest. She backed off a step or two before speaking. "How can you be thinking of food at a time like this?" she said accusingly.

"There's no sense in starving just because you're mad as hell at me," he observed with practicality. "Besides, what I have to say goes better with Chinese."

Allison caught herself before she chuckled and turned on him. "No!" she said, breathing the word like a curse. "You are not going to waltz your way back into my life with your corny jokes as if nothing had happened! And I am not mad at you," she claimed on a rising note of hysteria. "I just want you out of here once and for all!" She swung around and placed her hands on the kitchen counter for support, her breath coming in short, painful gasps. Why didn't he just go away and leave her alone?

"I wasn't trying to be funny," Cale said in a soft voice. "I've been trying to find a way to tell you . . . The words don't come easily for me, Allison." He stopped speaking. She thought for a moment he might have left the room, but she could sense he was still there behind her even if she couldn't see him. "I could really use that Scotch," he finally muttered, "and I think you could, too."

Cale quietly took it upon himself to find two glasses and poured each of them a good, stiff drink. He pressed one into her hand.

"Thank you," Allison murmured, and then nearly laughed. She was thanking him for pouring her a drink of her own Scotch. The whole situation was ludicrous. She might laugh if she were not so close to tears.

"Please, come sit down," he murmured, taking her by the arm and drawing her back into the living room.

They took seats at opposite ends of the sofa, seemingly absorbed in studying the contents of their glasses, neither willing to risk facing the other.

Cale took a large gulp of his Scotch, finishing it in one swoop. "I have been doing a lot of thinking the past few weeks," he began, then brought himself up short when he realized his drink was gone. He set the empty glass on the table beside the sofa and tried again. "In fact, all I've done for the past month is think, mostly about you." He glanced out of the corner of his eye to observe her reaction to this statement. He frowned when he apparently saw none. "I have been doing some serious thinking about my own life too." Cale gave a sigh and rearranged his arms and long legs, but no position seemed to provide the comfort he sought.

"We all need to reexamine our priorities from time to time," Allison said with a shrug, wishing he would get on with it, wondering where this was all headed.

"But don't you see—" He turned toward her, intensity written on his face. "It is possible to get so caught up in one way of thinking, one way of living, that sometimes it takes a near catastrophe to shake us out of our lethargy. Life is never static. It is always changing and we have to change with it. I was so caught up in the belief that my entire life revolved around writing, that I could only do that writing when I was alone, that I didn't discover until you were gone that it just isn't so. I haven't done a decent day's work since you left. It suddenly hit me that I need you to be with me. Not that I simply *want* you there, but that I actually *need* you to be there." Cale took a deep breath and waited for her response.

Allison finally turned to him. "What am I supposed to do? Cheer because you've discovered you can't do your all-precious writing without me?" The bitterness in her voice cut the air like a knife. "Well, bully for you, Cale Harding! So you're human, after all."

Cale was thrown off-balance temporarily by the utter contempt in her voice. Allison wondered if he expected her to fall into his arms with that pretty little speech. Well, if he did, then he had another think coming.

"I must have hurt you very badly, Allison." He sounded dismayed. "I know saying I'm sorry won't change that, but I am sorry."

"Save your sympathy, Cale. You need it far more than I do," she said, vexation passing over her face. If he started feeling sorry for her now, so help her God, he'd be out that door so fast his head would be spinning.

"Would it make any difference if I told you that I love you?" He went on then, a kind of desperation in his voice, "I'm in love with you, Allison, and I don't know what to do about it."

"Try a cold shower," she said sardonically. On the inside, she was a mass of violent tremors.

He ran his hands through his hair, unconsciously ruffling its brown mass, leaving him less than perfect and therefore more approachable. "I don't mean sex, although I can't deny I want you that way, too. I'm talking about love, about need, about seeing the rest of my life as a kind of walking death unless you're there to share it with me." Cale closed his eyes and Allison saw the shudder that ran down the entire length of his body.

Oh, God. She had wanted to hear those words from him more than life itself at one time. But did she want to hear them now? She loved him still, but there was a bitter edge to that love now. Could she forgive and forget?

"And when did you make this miraculous discovery?" she asked, throwing him a skeptical look.

Cale seemed to flinch. "I guess it was a gradual thing, noticing that food no longer had any taste, that sleep was elusive, that I didn't care about anything anymore if you weren't there. I suddenly saw no future for myself. I'm twenty-eight years old, Allison, but I feel like an old man."

She had been sitting there motionless, listening to every word he said, feeling the layer of ice around her heart begin to melt. How could she let pride stand in the way of her only chance for happiness? They both had come to the realization that they were in love, even if it had not been at the same moment.

"It's not that I don't love you, Cale. I never stopped loving you even for a moment, but I just don't know now." Her indecision seemed to light a spark of hope in him.

"Listen, honey." Cale moved closer to her and took one of her hands in his. "I know now that I was afraid to love you."

"Afraid to love me?" She sounded more than doubtful.

"You've got to understand, Allison, that everyone I've ever loved ended up leaving me. My father was killed when I was eleven years old. My grandmother died soon after I came back home after running away. And you know about my mother. I haven't had much practice at loving, but I know that I love you," he said, enfolding her in his arms and burying his face in her hair. "I need you desperately, Allison. Don't you know that I don't have a prayer without you?"

She didn't pull away, but neither did she put her arms around him in return. But, oh, how she had missed him, the feel of his strong arms around her, the uniquely masculine scent that was his, the caring touch of another human being. How could she carry bitterness in heart toward this man? She had to forgive and forget for her sake as well as for his.

Allison pulled back for a moment, trying to formulate the words of reconciliation that would heal the breach between them once and for all. "Cale, I—"

He interrupted her in a rush of words. "I'll get down on my knees and beg if I have to, Allison. Pride is a small price to pay, if it's my pride you want," he said in a hoarse voice. The words had been very difficult for him to say.

"No! Oh, Cale, no!" she cried out, throwing herself into his arms, knowing she could not ask that of him. Nothing else mattered now but that they loved each other. "I love you, Cale. I love you," she murmured over and over, seeking his mouth in the kiss that would begin to heal both their wounds.

"I love you, Allison," he said simply. But she knew now how much more was behind those three simple words.

Cale kissed her then with a kiss that foretold the love they would share in all the years to come. There was no room for bitterness in a heart filled with that kind of all-consuming love. A love that burned bright and hot, purifying the heart with its white heat.

They kissed and touched in the knowledge that they had very nearly lost each other and the rare passion that sprang up between them at the merest caress, the slightest touch. Allison met Cale's rising desire with her own, knowing that he loved her and she loved him. All else paled in comparison to that single fact.

She wrapped her arms tightly around him and held on for dear life as his mouth began to move over hers with equal shares of passion and tenderness. He not only wanted her this time, but loved and needed her as well. That made all the difference.

"Allison, honey—" Cale retreated from their kiss to gaze down into the eyes of the woman who lay in his arms. "I love you and I need you," he murmured in a husky voice. "I want you to be my wife."

"And I want you to be my husband, Cale Harding," she

repeated, as if it were a sacred vow. "I want to spend the rest of my life loving you."

This time when they came together, there was nothing to stand between them and the ultimate expression of that love—no doubts, no bitterness, no lingering hurt. They kissed as if a great thirst drove them. It was both a thirst and a hunger that could only be satisfied in the arms of the other. When they drew apart at last, both were breathless, their faces flushed, their bodies trembling.

Allison slowly got to her feet and held out her hand. "I want to make love with you, Cale Harding."

He rose to take the hand and the love she offered him. "And I want to love you as I never have before, Allison Saunders."

Allison led the way to her bedroom. She began to undress him with a light and loving touch. Cale followed her lead, easing the knit from her body, detouring along the way to caress a bare shoulder or a silky curve of skin.

They stood there in the center of the room for a moment, glorying in the sight of each other. Then Cale gently stretched her out on the bed and lay down beside her.

He reached for Allison as if in some part of his mind he had thought he would never find her in his arms again. He held her to him with a strength she knew would bind them for the rest of their lives. Then with each kiss, each caress, they felt that passion growing between them until it took over their minds as well as their bodies.

He found the rosy tips of her breasts and loved them until they curled up with pleasure into an expression of her growing desire. His hands played her body like an expert musician, instinctively knowing each touch that would excite and give pleasure. His fingers traced an erotic path

186

from breast to stomach to thigh, her unrestrained response to his touch beckoning him further.

Allison caressed his muscular, yet smooth, male body, realizing it would take a lifetime to learn all there was to know about this man. She touched the point of his passionate need and gently guided him toward her, wanting them to become as one, knowing this was the ultimate act of love. Cale eased himself down upon her, his tongue seeking the sweet nectar offered by her mouth as they joined together and indeed became one.

They moved together then, body pressed to body, glorying in their differences, yet with a single desire driving them to seek that final moment they would find in each other's arms. Soft, whispered words of love and desire and need were exchanged between mouths that never strayed far from each other and then only to caress a shoulder or the softness of a breast or the silky-smooth curve of a bare thigh.

Then the tender words were momentarily forgotten as passion demanded their complete attention. Cale fitted her legs around him, the surging rhythm of his lovemaking like ocean waves, until they met as a single entity, journeying as one as they reached the peak together.

They lay in each other's embrace without speaking for countless moments. When Cale finally eased his weight from Allison's body, it was only to gather her close to him.

All the words she wanted to hear from him seemed to pour forth now, as though some constraint had been lifted from his soul. They spoke long and in the low voices that lovers use until at last they slept.

Allison thought she was the first to awaken, but when she turned her head on the pillow she discovered Cale watching her with eyes that seemed to shine with love. "I love you," she mouthed, although no sound was forthcoming. She knew he heard her in the deepest recesses of his own heart.

"And I love and adore you," he murmured back, touching his lips to hers. Then Cale stretched his arms high above his head and folded them behind his neck, totally without self-consciousness that his body was stretched out in full view. "The second thing we have to do is look for that farm in Connecticut," he announced, as if he had been lying there beside her plotting their future while she slept.

"All right, I'll bite," Allison laughed, snuggling up beside him. "What's the first?"

"The first thing we have to do is go shopping for a bigger bed, my love," Cale answered with a coy smile. "I can't spend the rest of my life in these single beds you keep coming up with."

Allison chuckled from deep within her as she touched him in a loving caress. "A king-size bed for the king-size man in my life," she murmured, knowing it was her love that made him so.

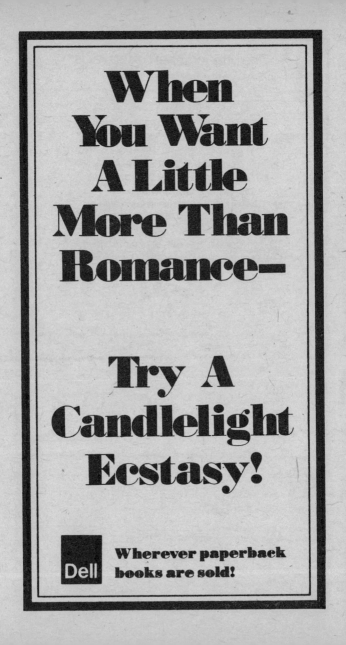

When
You Want
A Little
More Than
Romance—

Try A
Candlelight
Ecstasy!